I HAVE TO KNOW THEIR SECRET . . .

Why on earth would Joanna and her friends sneak out to the barn in the middle of the night to *sing?* Mia thought.

Then she realized the girls weren't singing at all, but chanting. The words sounded strange. Unfamiliar.

Mia felt her heart begin to beat with the pace and rhythm of the chant. The words seemed almost to reach through the door and wind themselves around her.

Mia took a step forward. Toward the door. Toward the sound. As if hypnotized by the repetition of the strange words.

A wave of dizziness washed over her. Why was her head spinning so?

She reached out to steady herself against the door. The wood felt warm and soft under her fingers. It feels like skin, Mia realized.

Then deep from inside the wood, a heart began to beat.

Circle of Fire

FEAR STREET Sagas®

R.L. Stine

#11

Circle of Fire

A Parachute Press Book

A GOLD KEY PAPERBACK
Golden Books Publishing Company, Inc.
New York

A GOLD KEY Paperback Original

Golden Books
888 Seventh Avenue
New York, NY 10106

ISBN: 0-307-24800-3

First Gold Key paperback printing March 1998

10   9   8   7   6   5   4   3   2   1

Cover art by Lisa Falkenstern

Printed in the U.S.A.

Circle of Fire

The Fear Family Curse

It began in fire . . .
. . . a raging fire that burned Susannah
Goode at the stake.

In 1662, Benjamin Fier, the magistrate of
Wickham Village, accused Susannah Goode of
possessing dark powers and sentenced her to
burn.

William Goode, Susannah's father, vowed
revenge on the Fier family. And while
Susannah was innocent in the ways of the
dark arts, her father was not. He summoned
the spirits of evil and asked them for justice.

"My hatred will live for generations,"
William promised. *"The fire that burned today
will not be quenched—until revenge is mine
and Fiers burn forever in the fire of my curse!"*

So the Fiers were cursed. And none has
escaped.

Simon Fier tried. A fortune-teller warned
him he was destined to burn to death—
because the letters of his name could be
rearranged to spell the word "fire." Simon
changed the spelling of his name to Fear, hoping to escape this horrible fate. But his
destiny was sealed. He died in a fire, and the
curse continued.

A curse so strong that it seeped into the
very ground where Simon Fear built his man-
sion, turning the quiet village of Shadyside
into a place of evil.

A curse so strong that it taints the life of
anyone who encounters a member of the
doomed Fear family.

Circle of Fire

. . . although I am somehow certain that this beloved book, with all its spells and secrets, will not be lost to future generations!

One day, another young woman of spirit shall discover the power within these precious pages. Too soon, I go to my grave. Having no daughter of my own, I use the last of my remaining power to beg that this knowledge not die with me. Only then shall I rest easy.

Emma Fier Reade
The Farmhouse
September 3, 1745

Emma laid down her quill pen. She blew softly across the wet ink as it dried on the thick pages of her journal.

Another shot of pain racked through her

1

body. Emma squeezed her eyes shut, refusing to cry out. She did not believe in showing weakness—any weakness. Even now, in her final hours of life, she refused to give in to feelings of hopelessness. One last task lay ahead.

Emma placed the journal in the deepest drawer of her writing desk. But the book—her precious book—demanded a more protected hiding place.

Emma lifted the book and hugged it briefly. She ran one thin, shaking hand across its soft leather cover. A feeling of deep comfort ran through her. She sighed, then forced herself to stand, to walk on unsteady legs across the sitting room floor. She stopped in the hall, turning to lock the door behind her. Then she made her way, slowly and painfully, to the stairs.

She climbed.

On the attic landing, a sudden cold, sharp, draft of wind pierced her to the bone. She gasped at the shock, clutching the book more tightly. Only a few minutes more, she promised herself. Then she could rest.

She pushed open the attic door and stood blinking while her eyes adjusted to the darkness. She scanned the room. There . . . there in the far corner, beneath that loose board . . . the perfect hiding place!

Emma kneeled. She tenderly kissed the book, then lowered it into the dark space. She pushed back the loose board to hide the secret compartment. A feeling of satisfaction swept through her. With the last of her strength, she forced herself to leave the attic. For the last time, she slowly made her way down the familiar stairs.

"**O**h, no," Mia Saxton whispered to herself as she raced down the hall toward the classroom. "I'm late again!"

She'd only been at Miss Pemberthy's School for Young Ladies for a few days, but she'd already been late twice. This would be the third time.

Mia simply couldn't get used to the class schedule. And it seemed impossible to find her way through the hallways and alcoves of the huge converted farmhouse.

This morning, Mia had reported to

English class and waited for ten minutes. Finally—when no one else arrived—she realized she was due in geography class, not English.

Mia rushed around the corner. Miss Pemberthy's nasal voice came drifting out of the doorway of the front parlor, where geography class was held.

"Girls, we're going to study the map of Europe today," she explained. "We'll begin with England, and then ... where is Miss Saxton?"

"Present, Miss Pemberthy." Mia skidded through the doorway so fast that she nearly tripped over the ruffled hem of her petticoat and long skirt.

Miss Pemberthy's long, narrow face was pinched with disapproval. "Late again, Miss Saxton?"

"I'm sorry," Mia murmured as she settled into her seat. She felt a drop of sweat roll down her forehead. I must look a sight, she thought.

"I hear that Miss Saxton is used to living on a farm," Alicia Bainbridge said in her haughty way. "Perhaps we should set the rooster to crow when it's time for geography."

The other girls tittered. Mia felt her

cheeks flame. Oh, how she hated it here!

She felt awkward and uncomfortable around girls like Alicia. Blond and pretty, Alicia had a wordly air that made her seem far older than her seventeen years. She wore the most fashionable gowns. Gowns her rich father could afford to buy her.

All the other girls looked up to Alicia. Whatever Alicia said to do, they did.

And Alicia had disliked Mia instantly.

Alicia dislikes almost everybody, Mia reminded herself. It's not just you.

But that didn't make her feel any better. Since Alicia disapproved of Mia, no one wanted to be her friend. No one even wanted to *talk* to her.

"Psst!" someone whispered. "Mia!"

Mia glanced over. Alicia had lifted her book so that it hid her mouth from Miss Pemberthy.

"Is that what they wear in Virginia these days?" Alicia looked disdainfully at Mia's dress. "It looks like something from 1825, not 1845! Here in Broad River, Louisiana, we try to be more up-to-date."

Mia didn't answer. She knew that whatever she said would be wrong.

Mia used to like the calico-print frock she

wore. She'd thought the high ruffle-neck collar and puffed sleeves were pretty. But now she knew her dress was completely out of style.

She wished—oh, how she wished—that her parents had the money to buy her silk gowns like Alicia's.

The blond girl smiled at Mia. "You're about the same size as my maid. Perhaps she could loan you something decent to wear."

Mia turned away and stared out the window. She couldn't bear to look at Alicia's sneering face.

Mia wished she could walk out of the classroom and leave the school forever. But there was no sense writing home requesting to leave Miss Pemberthy's. Her parents would simply tell her that they'd sent her here to get an education, not to make friends.

That's easy enough for them to say, she thought.

Her parents didn't have to be the stranger, the one no one wanted to talk to. And they didn't have to listen to Alicia's nasty remarks.

"Are you paying attention, Miss Saxton?" Miss Pemberthy asked.

"Yes, ma'am," Mia murmured. Miss

Pemberthy returned to her lecture, now talking about Belgium.

Mia began scribbling notes furiously. She was glad to set her mind on a country thousands of miles away. She didn't look up from her paper until Miss Pemberthy finished her lecture.

"You are dismissed, girls. You may go in to dinner now," Miss Pemberthy announced. "Remember, you are to study the map tonight. Tomorrow you will have a test on all the capitals of Europe."

Mia was sorry the lesson was over. Mealtimes were the worst part of the day for her. She felt so lonely eating in the big dining room with no one to talk to.

Mia gathered up her papers and followed the other girls into the hall. She saw that Alicia and her followers had formed a circle around a plump, short girl with frizzy hair caught up haphazardly in a loose bun. Clara Godert, Mia's roommate.

Poor Clara, Mia thought. She wasn't pretty or clever, and Alicia just loved to make fun of her.

"Clara, wherever did you have your hair styled?" Alicia cooed. "At the lunatic asylum, perhaps?"

Clara ducked her head. She didn't reply.

Say something back to her, Clara, Mia thought. Don't just stand there.

But she knew Clara didn't talk to *anyone*. Not even Mia. Mia had tried to start a conversation with her several times, but had gotten only a blank stare for her trouble.

Still, she couldn't just stand by and watch Alicia's cruelty. Mia walked down the hall toward the other girls. Alicia cast a glance over her shoulder and raised her perfect blond eyebrows.

"Why, it's the farm girl," she sneered.

Mia ignored her. "Clara, you promised to help me with the history lesson, remember?" she asked.

"I, ah—" Clara stammered.

"You won't get any help from *her*," Alicia said. "She doesn't even—"

"Oh, Clara's an excellent history student," Mia interrupted.

Alicia opened her mouth to say something else. But Miss Pemberthy came out of the classroom, and Alicia turned away. Mia breathed a sigh of relief.

"In to dinner, girls," the headmistress instructed with a sharp clap of her hands.

"Yes, Miss Pemberthy." Alicia smiled sweetly.

Mia waited until the headmistress passed her. Then she headed up the stairs to the small, third-floor bedroom she shared with Clara. She'd rather stay there than eat all by herself in the large main dining room again. Of course, she could eat with Clara, but Clara hadn't been all that friendly.

"Mia, please wait!" Clara called. Mia stopped on the staircase. This was the first time Clara had ever said more than two words to her.

Clara hurried onto the stairs. "Why did you do that?" she demanded.

"Why?" Mia repeated. "I'm simply tired of seeing Alicia pester you all the time. And I'd like for us to be friends."

"Friends? With me?" Clara asked. She sounded surprised.

Mia nodded. Clara studied her for what seemed like a long time. Then she nodded back. "Would you care to sit together at dinner?" she suggested.

"I would love to," Mia answered. She smiled. She'd finally made a friend!

Just before bedtime, Mia took the water pitcher down to the kitchen. She had one hand on the pump when a soft scraping sound caught her attention.

What's that? she wondered. She set down the pitcher and hurried to the door. She opened it and found a huge yellow tabby cat sitting on the porch.

"Goliath," she whispered fondly. "Begging again, you greedy, fat creature?"

The cat's yellow eyes almost seemed to glow in the dark. Of course he was begging. She'd been sneaking him scraps every night. He strolled into the kitchen.

"Miss Pemberthy will take the broom to you if she catches you inside," Mia whispered, bending to pet him.

He purred loudly, arching his back to meet her hand. She gave him the scraps of meat she'd hidden in her pocket. He gobbled hungrily, making purring-growly noises as he ate.

A board creaked behind her. With a gasp, Mia whirled to face the sound. To her relief, she saw Clara standing in the doorway.

"You scared me half to death," Mia exclaimed.

Clara cast a glance over her shoulder, then came into the room to pet the cat.

"He's so pretty." She looked up at Mia. "So this is where you sneak off to every night."

"I miss having animals around," Mia confessed. Then she smiled as an idea rushed into her head. "Why don't we take him upstairs for a bit? I can sneak him outside again when everyone's asleep."

Clara returned her grin. "I'd like that."

They managed to get the cat up to their room without anyone seeing them. Mia was glad to see Clara and Goliath get along so well. Now Clara had two friends.

When the hall clock chimed eleven, Mia tucked Goliath under her arm. "I better take him back," she whispered to Clara.

Mia sneaked out into the quiet, dimly lit hall. Tiptoeing past closed bedroom doors, she made her way to the shadowy kitchen.

Cold winter air poured into the room as she opened the door, blowing in a few snowflakes with it. When she gently dropped Goliath outside, he ran back in, making it clear that he preferred the warm kitchen.

"You lazy thing," Mia murmured, rubbing his ears. "You're supposed to be hunting mice in the barn."

She carried him out and set him on the

porch steps. He looked at her reproachfully for a moment before stalking off into the snow-covered garden.

Then he stopped. His ears went back. A low growl rumbled in his throat as he stared at the barn.

"What's the matter, boy?" Mia asked.

Then she saw it.

Something stood beside the barn.

Something with huge, dark wings.

Mia stepped back into the shadows. What is it? she thought. What is that thing?

Mia heard the huge wings flap. She gasped with terror as she realized that the creature was turning.

And it was going to see her.

Chapter Two

Mia could feel her heart thudding against her ribs. Could she duck back into the school before the creature saw her?

The barn door swung open. Light spilled across the dark, winged creature.

It's a girl! Mia realized. It's just a girl! The wings had been nothing but the girl's long, full cloak blowing in the wind.

Mia peered at the girl's face. Joanna Kershaw! Joanna was Alicia's chief rival for leadership among the students.

"What are you doing out here so late, Joanna?" Mia murmured to herself. Another girl appeared in the barn doorway and beckoned Joanna inside.

Joanna paused for a moment, glancing all around as if to make sure no one was watching. Then she slipped inside. The barn door closed behind her.

Mia scratched her cheek thoughtfully. Joanna had her own group of followers. They mostly stayed to themselves, ignoring the other girls. Mia had assumed they simply thought of themselves as better than everyone else. But obviously something else was going on.

What could they be doing? Why were they sneaking out to the barn in the middle of the night? Mia wondered.

Of course, they must be doing something they didn't want anyone to know about. It had to be something so forbidden even their rooms didn't offer enough privacy.

Mia's curiosity soared. She would just die if she didn't find out what they were doing in the barn. Impulsively, she ran out into the yard. The snow crunched under her high-buttoned shoes as she crossed to the barn.

When she reached the barn door, she was surprised to see that no light shone from under it. Surely Joanna and the other girl weren't sitting in the dark. Where had they gone? Had they slipped out the back door of the barn?

She lifted the iron latch and the door swung open silently. The barn was dark and still.

One of the horses in the stalls whinnied softly at her. "Shhh," she whispered, stroking the animal's silky neck. "Easy. We don't want them to know I'm here."

Reassured, the horse nibbled at her hair. Mia patted his neck once more. She inhaled, smelling horses and fresh hay. Familiar. Expected. But beneath those odors she detected the scent of candles burning. She went looking for the source of the candle smoke.

She followed that scent to the tack room at the rear of the barn. The door was closed. Faint light flickered through the boards. Mia could hear voices now, several of them. They were singing. Softly, almost in a whisper.

Why on earth would Joanna and her friends sneak out to the barn in the middle of the night to *sing*?

Then Mia realized that they weren't singing at all, but chanting. The words sounded strange. Unfamiliar.

Mia crept closer.

She could hear them more clearly now. But she still couldn't understand what they were saying.

The chant wasn't in English. Or French or German or even Latin. It wasn't any language she'd ever heard. The words were sharp. They cut off abruptly at the end of each syllable.

Mia felt her heart begin to beat with the pace and rhythm of it. The words seemed almost to reach through the door and wind themselves around her.

"What is this?" she whispered.

Mia took a step forward. Toward the door. Toward the sound. As if hypnotized by the repetition of the strange words.

She reached for the door handle. And her fingers began to tingle.

Mia shook her hands, and the warm, tingling feeling shot through her body like heat lightning. She gasped softly.

It was the chant! The chant was doing this to her. She knew it, although she didn't know how she knew it. It was as if a deep, long-forgotten knowledge was stirring within her.

The chant itself seemed to pump through her veins with every beat of her heart.

The tingling grew stronger. Stronger still. Filling her body.

She had to get away from there.

Mia turned to run. A wave of dizziness washed over her. She teetered, almost fell.

Why was her head spinning so?

She reached out to steady herself against the door. The wood felt warm and soft under her fingers. It feels like skin, Mia realized.

Then, from deep inside the wood, a heart began to beat.

Chapter Three

I can't be feeling a heartbeat in the door, Mia thought. I can't. It's impossible.

My own heart is pounding so hard I can feel it in my fingertips, she decided. That is the only explanation.

Mia pressed her hand more firmly against the door. It flew open. She tumbled into the room and landed on the rough, planked floor.

She realized the chanting had stopped. The tingling, burning sensation in her body had disappeared.

Mia shook her hair back from her face and looked up.

Joanna and three other girls had gathered around her. Mia put names to faces: Phoebe Dixon, Irene Weathersby, Anabel Tritt—Joanna's whole group of followers.

Mia pushed herself to her feet. Joanna moved in front of the doorway, blocking her escape.

Joanna clutched a tattered, leather-bound book protectively in her arms. It was ancient-looking. "What are you doing here?" Joanna demanded. She tossed back her mane of red curls.

"N-nothing," Mia stammered. "I wasn't doing anything. I was just . . ." She let her voice trail off. She was too astounded by the sight before her to say another word.

Tall, black candles burned everywhere, on shelves and boxes, some stuck to the floor with melted wax. Someone had used charcoal to draw a circle on the rough planks of the floor. Inside the circle was drawn a strange, eight-sided symbol. Mia had never seen anything like it.

In the center of the symbol sat a wedge-shaped piece of gray metal. Its sides were inscribed with swirling designs.

Mia felt the hair at the back of her neck stand on end. There was something repellent about the odd symbol and the piece of metal. Something *wrong*.

But, like the chant, the symbol felt somehow . . . familiar.

"Well?" Joanna prompted. "Did someone send you here to spy on us?"

Mia shook her head. "I wasn't spying. I just happened to see you come out here, and I followed."

"She's going to tell," Irene said.

"No!" Mia protested. "I don't care what you're doing. I only want to leave."

The girls wore identical expressions of suspicion. Even Irene, who usually had a smile on her sweet, round face.

Joanna clutched the book she held to her chest. "And why should we believe you? We don't even know you."

Mia opened her mouth to speak, but no words came out. Her pulse felt like a drumroll in her ears. The strange dizziness was returning. And the tingling! It was starting again in her fingertips.

Mia rubbed her palms against her skirt. But the tingling grew stronger.

"Look!" Anabel cried. Her hand trembled as she pointed toward the charcoal symbol on the floor.

The symbol was moving. Throbbing.

It couldn't be, Mia thought. It had to be a trick of the light.

But deep down inside, she knew it was no trick.

"What is it?" Joanna cried, alarm turning her voice shrill. "What's happening?"

All at once, the candle flames bent toward Mia. Every one of them. Bowing. The sizzle of burning wax filled the room.

All eyes locked on Mia.

Mia drew in a sharp breath. Why was this happening? Why were the flames flickering in her direction? She had no part in this.

Then Phoebe uttered a long, shrill scream.

The girls followed Phoebe's horrified gaze to the center of the tack room. There, in the middle of the pulsing charcoal drawing, the metal wedge glowed red. As if heated by some inner flame.

Slowly, it began to turn.

Still turning, it rose into the air.

Mia heard the others gasp, but she could not tear her gaze away from that glowing piece of metal.

It continued to spin. Around and around, faster and faster.

Then it stopped. Hanging in empty air.

And it pointed straight at Mia.

Chapter Four

Why is it pointing at me? Mia panicked.

The metal pointer fell to the ground. Mia couldn't stop staring at it. What just happened?

"Did . . . did we do that?" Irene asked.

"I didn't think it would actually work. I thought it was just a game," Phoebe said.

"Mia, it's you!" Joanna said, her voice shaking.

Mia jerked her head up and blinked.

Joanna raised her hand and pointed her finger at Mia. Her whole arm trembled. "You did this," she said.

Mia didn't know what Joanna was talking about. And she didn't want to find out. She wanted to go back to her room and forget this ever happened.

"I—I have to leave. I won't tell anyone anything. I promise," Mia stammered.

Joanna didn't move from her position in front of the door. "Here, let me show you something." She opened the ancient-looking book and held it out to Mia. "Look," she ordered.

A black-and-white ink etching covered the first page. The etching showed five girls sitting in a circle around a symbol just like the one on the tack-room floor. A metal wedge had been drawn to appear floating over their heads.

Almost against her will, Mia reached out and touched the page.

She drew her hand back sharply.

Touching the page had sent that tingling thrill racing up her arm. The same pins-and-needles sensation she'd felt at the door, and just before the drawing on the floor began to throb.

"What is it?" she asked, her voice quaking.

"It's a book of spells," Joanna told her.

She sounds so calm, Mia thought. How can she sound so calm?

"I found it up in the attic last month," Joanna said. "We've been trying to use it."

Phoebe came to Joanna's side. Her pale skin was even paler after the event she'd just witnessed. She twirled a strand of her blond hair around her finger.

"We tried and tried to work the spells, but nothing ever happened," Phoebe explained.

She glanced at Joanna with a guilty expression on her face. "I never thought anything would," she said. "But Miss Pemberthy's is so stuffy. And I thought it would be fun to sneak out. I didn't expect . . ."

Joanna frowned at Phoebe. "I never would have asked you to join the circle if I knew you thought it was a joke." Phoebe returned Joanna's frown with a defiant look.

She turned her attention back to Mia. Her green eyes glittered excitedly. "You made the difference, Mia. You have to help us."

Mia shook her head. "I can't—"

"You have to!" Joanna insisted. "For some odd reason, the spells won't work without you. That's why the metal wedge floated up and pointed at you. That's what it must have been telling us."

Joanna pointed to the drawing. "Look. This picture depicts five girls. It might be that our spells didn't work because there were only four of us. Mia completes the circle."

"Why didn't we think of that before?" Anabel asked.

"Needing the fifth girl makes sense," Mia said.

"Maybe we should forget the whole thing," Irene said softly. She wrapped her arms around her body. Mia could see that she was trembling.

"You agreed to do this, Irene," Joanna snapped.

"I know. But I never believed . . ." Irene shook her head. "I never believed anything would really happen."

"And now that it has, you're afraid?" Joanna demanded. "This is one of the most exciting things that has ever happened to any of us."

Joanna pushed the book of spells into

Mia's hands. "Help us," she urged, clutching Mia's wrist. "You must."

She glanced at the other three girls.

"Please, Mia," Phoebe begged. "Aren't you curious? I am."

"Isn't there anything you want?" Anabel asked Mia. "Who knows what the spells might be able to give us."

"I'm not sure," Mia stammered.

Irene stared down at the metal wedge. Finally she raised her eyes and looked at Mia. "I'll do it if you will," she whispered.

Mia became aware of a change in the air. It felt thick and charged, like the air just before a storm.

The tingling sensation grew stronger than ever before. Mia's fingers started to shake. She dropped the book.

Joanna dropped to her knees to pick it up, but froze.

The metal wedge was once again rising into the air. Anabel gasped and clutched Mia's hand.

The wedge began to spin, faster and faster until the pointer became a blur. The inscriptions on its sides began to glow.

We're doing that! Mia thought. We're causing it to spin like that.

It was impossible, incredible . . . but it was true. She could feel an echo of that hot, red glow flowing through her veins.

Light burst from the charcoal symbol on the floor. Eerie, blue-white flames licked along the outlines of the design.

Mia reacted with a farm girl's quickness about fire and barns. She grabbed a water bucket and doused the flames. To her surprise, she saw that the floor wasn't even scorched.

"We have power together," Joanna said. "I was right."

Mia stared down at the symbol. It seemed so innocent now, just a drawing in charcoal. But they had made it burn. Oh, yes. She couldn't deny it. She'd felt the power running through her body.

She had to know how strong this new power was. She had to know what she could do.

"Yes," she told them. "I'll join you."

"Oh, good!" Phoebe cried. Her blue eyes burned with excitement. "Let's try something else right away."

Joanna shook her head. "It's nearly midnight. We'd better get back before someone misses us. But first, we have to swear that we'll never tell anyone else about these secret meetings."

"Swear?" Anabel asked. "How?"

Joanna held the book of spells out in front of her. "Put one hand on this," she ordered.

Anabel, Phoebe, and Irene obeyed. Mia hesitated just for a moment. Then she too placed her hand on the book. She felt it grow warm beneath her palm. She checked the faces of the others for a reaction. No one else seemed aware of the sensation she felt.

"Now, repeat after me," Joanna told them. "By the power of the spell book, we swear never to tell anyone about our meetings or what we do in them. Whoever breaks this oath will suffer terrible punishment. No matter how far she runs, no matter where she hides, the power will find her."

Joanna stared at Mia expectantly. Although all Mia's instincts warned her against taking such an oath, she knew it was too late to back out now.

Besides, these girls were going to be her friends. She had to help them.

So she repeated Joanna's words along with the others. As she did, the tingle swept from her fingertips and spread throughout her body.

She'd claimed the power. Or maybe, a small voice whispered in her mind, the power had claimed her.

"Joanna, what will happen to anyone who breaks the vow?" Irene asked. She sounded nervous.

"I don't know," Joanna told her. "Maybe she'd burn up in that blue-white fire. Maybe she'd be turned into an animal or a tree. Maybe she'd just disappear. Whichever, I know I'd never, ever take that chance."

Phoebe giggled. "This is so thrilling!"

"Isn't it!" Anabel agreed in a breathy, excited voice.

They swept the charcoal mark off the floor and blew the candles out. Then they hurried through the snowy yard and slipped back into the house through the kitchen door.

Joanna took the lead as they sneaked single file up the stairs. Mia was last.

"We will all eat together tomorrow at breakfast," Joanna whispered when they reached the second-floor landing. "You as well, Mia."

Phoebe giggled under her breath. "Yes, and don't be late. Alicia and her friends always gobble up all the biscuits if they can!"

Mia laughed happily, clapping her hand over her mouth to stifle the sound. She was one of them now! Even though she'd been really frightened tonight, it was worth it.

The others moved ahead up the stairs to their bedrooms on the third floor. Mia began to follow, but stopped short. She had the feeling she was forgetting something.

The water pitcher! I left it in the kitchen, she realized.

She had to go back and get it. She turned around—and gasped.

"Oh, no! It can't be!"

Chapter Five

"**W**hat exactly are you girls doing?" Miss Pemberthy demanded.

"I told you I heard some girls sneaking around outside." Alicia simpered.

"Thank you, Alicia," the headmistress replied. She smiled at her pet student.

The headmistress pinned Mia and the others with a forbidding glare. "Now I want to know what you girls were doing outside at this hour."

Mia glanced at the others and saw her

own dread mirrored in their faces. They were in big trouble now. There was no excuse good enough for going out without permission.

Joanna hurried down the stairs and stood next to Mia. "We didn't mean any harm by it, Miss Pemberthy," she explained. "It was only a silly game. We dared one another, and before we knew it, there we were."

Alicia rolled her eyes.

Miss Pemberthy crossed her arms. "I trust you enjoyed your little escapade?" she asked.

"Yes, Ma'am," Anabel told her. "I mean, no, Ma'am." A deep blush covered Anabel's cheeks.

The headmistress nodded sharply. "Very well. Now that you have had your fun, you ladies will have the job of washing dishes after each meal for the next two days."

"But, Miss Pemberthy—" Phoebe wailed. "We're not kitchen help!"

"Nevertheless," the headmistress continued, "you will wash the pots and pans and make sure both the kitchen and the dining room are spotless. The help will enjoy a short vacation."

"Yes, Ma'am," Irene said quickly.

"But that's not fair!" Anabel protested.

"You would prefer that I write your parents?" Miss Pemberthy inquired.

"No, Ma'am," Anabel muttered.

"Very well. Dishes it will be. Beginning at breakfast tomorrow, girls. And I don't expect to hear another peep out of any of you tonight." Miss Pemberthy turned and strode away.

The moment the headmistress had moved out of earshot, Joanna turned to Alicia. "You snake," Joanna whispered. "You ought to keep your nose out of other people's business."

"I put my nose wherever I please," Alicia retorted. "And you can't do a thing about it. My father is the richest man in the state, and don't you think that Miss Pemberthy ever forgets it!"

The two girls glared at each other. Then Joanna whirled around and stomped off to her room.

Mia sighed and started up the stairs. She glanced over her shoulder at Alicia. The blond girl smiled, gloating over the trouble she'd caused.

"Horrible creature," Mia muttered under

her breath. She hurried down the hall and tiptoed into her room. She didn't want to wake Clara.

But Clara sat up when Mia came in. She looked worried.

"Where were you?" she demanded. She pushed her hair away from her face. "I waited and waited, but you never came back. I even went downstairs looking for you. You weren't even in the house!"

Mia swallowed hard, wishing she could tell Clara what had happened. After all, Clara was her friend, the first one she'd made here. But she'd sworn not to tell anyone, and she couldn't break that oath.

"I . . . went out somewhere," she said.

"Where?"

Mia sighed. She felt horribly uncomfortable about this, but there was nothing she could do.

"I can't tell you," she replied. "I'm sorry, Clara. But I gave my word not to tell anyone."

"Oh," Clara mumbled. "That's all right."

It wasn't all right, Mia could tell. She'd hurt Clara's feelings.

But no matter how bad she might feel about it, she still couldn't tell. So she just said good night and crawled into bed.

As she drifted off to sleep, she thought of the perfect solution to the problem. She'd ask the others if Clara could join the group!

Even if Clara couldn't actually participate in the spells, she could act as a lookout or something, Mia thought. At least she'd be included.

"Miss Pemberthy is wrong if she thinks this is going to stop us," Joanna defiantly told the others after breakfast the next morning. She plunged a stack of dishes into a basin of soapy water.

"But . . . if we get caught again . . . we'll be sent home," Irene said haltingly.

"Then we will be careful not to get caught again," Joanne insisted.

"We can't stop now," Phoebe said. "Aren't you curious? I know I am!"

"What we are doing is too amazing," Anabel agreed.

"You don't want to stop, do you Mia?" Joanna stared at her.

"No," Mia said. "I agreed to help you, and I will."

Mia handed Joanna another pile of dirty dishes. "I've got something to ask all of you. It's about Clara. Can she join our group?"

"Clara *Godert*?" Anabel demanded.

"Not her!" Irene exclaimed.

"Give her a chance," Mia pleaded. "She really is nice if you take the time to get to know her."

Joanna shook her head. "No. Absolutely not. The spell book shows five girls. If four wouldn't work, neither will six."

"But even if she doesn't help with the spells, she could be a lookout for us," Mia protested.

"No," Joanna insisted. "We can't trust just anyone with our secret. Don't you agree, girls?"

"We agree," they chorused.

Mia looked around at their faces. She didn't understand why they were so set against having Clara. But it was obvious that it wouldn't do any good to argue further.

"We'll meet in the barn at eleven," Joanna announced.

When Mia heard the clock strike the quarter hour, she slipped out of bed. It was almost time to meet the others.

Mia quickly dressed. She glanced over at Clara. Good. She was still asleep.

Mia eased open the door and checked the hall. Empty.

She crept out and softly shut the door behind her. Then she tiptoed down to the kitchen.

When she opened the door to the back porch, she found Goliath waiting. "Poor kitty. It's freezing tonight," she murmured. She tossed him the dinner scraps from her pocket as she hurried past.

The light of a half moon lit her path to the barn. She found Joanna and the others sitting in a circle when she arrived. The flickering candlelight cast deep shadows across their faces.

"Take your place in the circle," Joanna ordered. "It's time to start."

Mia sat down between Irene and Anabel. She noticed that Irene kept nervously twisting the hem of her skirts into knots.

"Which spell should we try?" Phoebe asked.

Joanna set the book on the floor in front of her. She opened it to the first spell. Mia leaned over to see it more closely.

The spell had been written in the form of

a poem, or the stanzas of a song. None of the words were familiar. The ink was an odd, brownish-red color.

Like old blood, Mia thought.

"This doesn't say what the spell is for," Mia said.

"None of them do," Joanna replied. "We've just been repeating the words exactly, hoping that something would work."

The hair rose on the nape of Mia's neck. "You're joking, surely!" she exclaimed. "You can't just chant, not knowing what might happen?"

"Are you afraid?" Joanna challenged.

Mia was. But she didn't want to admit it. She had finally made some new friends. She wanted them to like her.

Don't be silly, she chided herself. Nothing bad is going to happen.

"Why don't we just start with the first spell?" Mia suggested. "Maybe it will be one for magically washing dishes!"

The others laughed. Even timid Irene.

Joanna took a piece of charcoal out of her pocket. "Whose turn is it?" she asked.

"Mine," Anabel told her.

Joanna handed her the charcoal, then

closed the spell book so that Anabel could see the design on the cover. Anabel began to draw.

Mia clenched her hands nervously as she watched the design take shape. It was as if she could feel the dark magic entering the room with every stroke of the charcoal. Finally, Anabel finished.

"Everybody join hands," Joanna instructed.

They obeyed. Irene's fingers felt like ice against Mia's hand. She's afraid, too, Mia thought.

Joanna opened the book to the first spell, then propped it up where they could all see the pages.

"Remember," she told them. "Say the words exactly as they are written."

"I wish we knew what they meant," Irene said.

"It doesn't matter what they mean," Joanna replied. "As long as they work. Ready, everyone?"

They all nodded. Mia took a good, tight grip on her friends' hands and started chanting. The words felt strange in her mouth.

Her fingers started to tingle. The same

awful sensation she'd felt the night before. The tingling spread. It ran up her arms and settled in her chest.

Just as it had yesterday, the rhythm of the chant seeped into her bones, her blood.

Only tonight she didn't fight it. Last night she'd been terrified. Now, she was still scared, but everything had changed. Tonight she was no longer a stranger. She was part of this group. And she had promised to help.

Mia knew she had to let the feeling take her where it would.

A harness began to quiver on its hook, bouncing its brass buckle against the wall. Mia jerked in surprise.

Something is happening!

Beads of sweat dotted Phoebe's upper lip. Anabel's grip tightened on Mia's hand, hurting her. But Mia couldn't let go. She couldn't let go until the spell was finished.

Nails jittered on the work-table. Then the tools began to rattle. The reins hanging on the walls began to swing.

Mia saw one of the candles on the clos-est crate tremble. It shook harder and harder, until it bounced onto the floor. The flame hissed out in a puddle of melted wax.

But the candle kept moving. It rolled from side to side, over and over. In time with the chant, Mia realized. She felt her stomach turn over.

Pieces of hay rolled across the floor. One stood up on end, whirling like a top. A tin bucket shuddered, then lurched over onto its side.

Excitement raced like lightning through Mia. She'd never dreamed this could happen.

We're doing this! she thought.

Power. They were using the power of the spell book. They could make things happen, incredible things.

A mouse scurried across the floor. It raced along the edge of the crate, and headed for the feed bags at the far end of the room.

Then it stopped. It stood completely still.

Mia stared at it. The only time she'd seen a mouse do that was when it was being stalked by a cat. Sometimes, when a mouse could see no other way out, it would play dead.

The mouse slowly began to move again. It turned one way, then the other. The tiny creature rose onto its hind legs. It held its front paws tightly against its furry chest.

Mia heard Irene give a low whimper as the mouse began to dance. Twirling, whirling, whiskers twitching, it danced to the rhythm of the chant.

We're controlling it, Mia thought. We're making it dance.

"Look!" Anabel cried. "Look at that mouse!"

Her voice broke Mia's concentration. She stumbled over the next word in the chant.

All movement in the barn stopped. Everything went still. The sudden silence almost seemed to echo. Mia's throat felt tight and strange, and she had to swallow to clear it.

The mouse dropped down on all fours. Mia waited for it to scurry away, but it just sat there, its sides heaving. Its mouth opened wide. As if . . . as if it were trying to scream.

She stared at the creature's wide-open mouth. Was it in pain? Had they hurt the little thing?

"No, it was only a dance!" she whispered. "We didn't hurt it, only made it dance! We only—"

She broke off with a gasp as the mouse rolled over onto its side. All four legs stuck stiffly out. The small, pink mouth stretched still wider.

And then the mouse went still.

Mia jumped to her feet. "It's dead!" she cried. "We killed it!"

Chapter Six

"**M**ia's right. We killed it. I—I knew we shouldn't . . ." Irene mumbled.

"Oh, don't be such babies," Joanna said irritably. "It's only a mouse. Besides, you can't be sure it's dead."

Mia stared down at the mouse. Its beady eyes stared back at her glassily.

"It *looks* dead," Irene said.

Joanna picked up a stick and leaned over the mouse. She poked it gingerly. It didn't move.

"We didn't know what the spell would

do," Mia said softly. "We didn't think it could be dangerous."

The mouse gave a high-pitched squeal. It scrambled to its feet.

Mia jerked back. Phoebe screeched.

The mouse raced away across the floor.

"Oh, good gracious," Irene gasped, her hand over her heart. "That nearly frightened me to death!"

Anabel and Phoebe nodded.

"Me too," Mia said. "But at least it is all right."

Joanna snorted. "Danger, indeed! If our spell won't hurt even a tiny mouse, we have no cause for concern. Isn't that so, Mia?"

"Well, I . . ." Mia let her voice trail away.

Joanna frowned at her. Mia knew she expected nothing less than total agreement. "I suppose not," Mia agreed reluctantly.

"That's what I've been telling you," Joanna stated with a superior smile. "Now that we've recovered from that little scare, let us try another spell."

Joanna flipped through the book, finally settling on a spell near the back. "This looks interesting," she said. "Ready, everyone?"

Anabel took Mia's hand again, and Mia

took Irene's. Mia gazed down at the ancient words on the yellowed page. This spell was longer and more complicated.

What is it going to do? Mia thought.

"Begin," Joanna said. And they began to chant.

The words were shorter and harsher. Mia stumbled over the rhythm, not feeling comfortable with it.

She glanced at the others. They didn't seem to be having any trouble.

They began the second verse of the chant. The familiar tingle ran up her hands. It continued up the back of her neck and down her spine. The tingle finally centered itself in the middle of her forehead.

Mia heard the wind begin to blow and lifted her gaze to the window. The wind whipped at the trees. Their winter-bare limbs rasped against the side of the barn like dry bones.

Then Mia noticed something that made her heart pound. The trees farther away from the barn stood straight and still. No wind blew through their branches.

The wind belongs to us, Mia thought. We brought it to life with our chant. A shudder raced through her.

Mia returned her gaze to the spell book. Wait. She had been chanting while she stared out the window. That meant she had been chanting without reading the words. Chanting words she had never spoken in her life!

The buzzing, pulsing tingle in her forehead grew stronger.

Mia looked at the others. They chanted, their expressions calm. They didn't seem to hear the wind sobbing against the windowpanes as though begging to be let in. They didn't appear to feel the horrible tingling.

Maybe we should stop, Mia thought. What if something bad happens?

But her lips continued to speak the strange words. The rhythm of the chant filled her. Urging her on.

Mia realized she was terribly cold. Freezing wind was seeping into the barn through openings in the wooden plank walls.

She kept chanting. The spell was almost finished now.

The wail of the wind deepened. The trees near the barn thrashed back and forth in the gale.

A roaring filled Mia's ears. Was it the wind, or the power inside her? The other girls' voices grew faint, as though they came from far away.

One more line remained of the spell. Mia didn't have to look at the book to speak the words. Her gaze remained fixed on the window.

Shadows gathered near the biggest tree. Bending and twisting. Growing and stretching until they were a little taller than a man.

The shadows are forming something, Mia realized.

Two bright silver flecks appeared in the shadows. Moonlight? she wondered.

No, eyes.

Then she knew what they had done. The spell. It had been a call. A summons.

And something had answered.

Chapter Seven

"**S**top!" Mia cried, forcing the sound from her dry throat.

The candle flames flickered wildly. Then they went out. Darkness claimed the room.

Irene screamed.

They hadn't spoken the last words. The spell hadn't been finished!

Mia hoped it wasn't too late. She knew she had to look out the window, to know for certain if they'd stopped in time. But she was afraid. So afraid.

What if . . . when she looked out, it was looking back at her?

Mia raised her eyes to the window. The shadow creature was gone.

The trees were still. The howling wind had stopped.

"Someone get a match," Joanna commanded.

Mia's hands trembled uncontrollably. She clenched her fists to stop the shaking, but it helped only a little.

You are all right, she told herself. You are safe. You are all safe.

Phoebe struck a match and began to relight the candles.

"Mia! What happened? Why did you stop the spell?" Anabel demanded.

"You spoiled it!" Joanna accused.

"Didn't you see what was out there?" Mia cried. "Couldn't you hear the wind crying? Didn't any of you have any idea of what was happening out there? Didn't you feel it?"

"Feel what?" Joanna asked, bewildered.

"We were calling something . . . and something was answering. Something *wrong*," Mia answered. "Something evil."

"Oh, Mia," Irene whispered.

"It took shape right in front of my eyes. I don't think it was fully formed before I stopped the chant," she continued, speaking fast and breathlessly. "But who knows what it was or what it would have done. And none of us had the slightest idea of how to control it. I had to stop the spell before the creature became complete. I had to!"

Joanna stared at her for a moment. Then she scowled. "Mia Saxton, you're making this all up. You got scared and ruined the spell, plain and simple."

"That's not so," Mia protested.

"Yes, it is," Joanna insisted. "You were scared, and now you're making up a silly story to excuse yourself. Well, we're not going to allow it!"

She snatched the book up from the floor and stalked out of the tack room. The door banged closed behind her.

"But I *saw* it!" Mia cried, turning to the others.

"Then why didn't any of us see anything?" Anabel asked. "I noticed you looking out the window and I looked, too. I didn't see a thing."

"You didn't even see the trees blowing?" Mia pressed.

Anabel shrugged. "That's not the sort of thing I'd notice. It's winter. Trees blow sometimes. I certainly didn't see any evil fiend. I don't know what *you* saw."

"I don't know, either," Mia replied miserably. "Neither of you saw anything?" she asked Phoebe and Irene.

They both shook their heads.

"Maybe I did let my imagination run away with me," Mia said. "Maybe all I saw was shadows. Maybe the wind was just wind."

"Don't worry, it will be all right," Irene told her. "Joanna's angry with you, but she'll forget it by tomorrow."

Mia was glad the other girls weren't angry at her, too. She helped them gather up the candles and sweep the charcoal design from the floor. It only took a few minutes to clean everything up.

Anabel took a last look around. "We'd better get back before that Alicia starts snooping. She'd love to tattle on us again."

Mia grabbed her cloak and led the way. She opened the barn door and looked out to make sure no one was watching. Clouds covered the moon.

What if that thing is not really gone? she

thought. What if it is hiding out there. Waiting for them.

"Hurry up," Phoebe whispered. "It's freezing."

Mia stepped out into the yard. She nearly ran into Joanna. "I thought you went back already," Mia said.

Joanna didn't turn. She didn't seem to notice that Mia had spoken to her. She stood motionless beside the tree closest to the barn.

The clouds floated away from the moon. Cold silver light spilled across the ground. Mia's insides turned to ice.

Now she knew why Joanna had stopped. Now she knew why Joanna was acting so strangely.

Great slashes marked the trunk of the tree. The wood gleamed white beneath the shredded remains of bark.

Those are claw marks, Mia thought. Something clawed that tree. Something huge.

Chapter Eight

"Mia was right," Anabel stammered. "She . . . she really *did* see something!"

"I told you," Mia whispered.

"Is it still out here?" Phoebe whispered.

Mia shook her head. "I don't know. I don't think so. I think it disappeared when we stopped the chant."

She touched Joanna's shoulder lightly. "Are you all right?"

"Yes . . . I'm fine," she answered.

But Mia could hear the tremble in Joanna's voice. And when Joanna pushed a stray lock of red hair back from her face, Mia noticed her hand shaking.

"Let's go back in the barn," Mia suggested. "We have to talk about this."

They hurried back inside. No one objected when Phoebe lit the lamp that hung just inside the door.

For a moment, they stood in silence, looking at one another. No one seemed to know what to say.

"You were right to stop the spell, Mia," Joanna said finally. "It was more than we could handle just now."

Just now? Mia swallowed, remembering those slashes on the tree. She didn't think she'd ever be able to handle that. Or want to!

"I don't want to do this anymore," she told them.

"Maybe Mia is right," Irene said.

Joanna glared at her. "I'll keep going if everyone else wants to," Irene added quickly.

"We can't stop," Joanna protested. "Remember, the first spell wasn't bad. It didn't even hurt that mouse."

"Yes!" Phoebe agreed excitedly. "Tonight's spell came from the back of the book. I kept thinking it was more complicated than any of the others we tried."

Joanna nodded. "The spells in the beginning of the book *are* shorter and simpler. If we stick to those, we won't have any trouble. When we have more experience, we can try the more complicated ones."

"Please, Mia?" Anabel begged.

What Joanna said made some sense. But Mia didn't like the idea of taking the chance again. "What if something horrible happens?" she asked.

"What if it doesn't?" Anabel countered.

Mia sighed. If she stopped, they'd have to stop, too. It wouldn't be fair. Besides, Joanna was right. Nothing bad had happened when they'd cast that first spell. They should be all right if they stayed with the simple ones.

And you want to learn to use the power, Mia thought. You want to control it. Admit it.

"All right," Mia told them. "But we have to do the spells in order."

"Agreed," Joanna answered.

With that settled, Mia and the others

hurried back to the house and sneaked upstairs. Clara was still sleeping when Mia slipped into the room they shared.

Mia undressed and slid under the covers. She lay awake for a long time, listening to Clara's soft breathing.

She felt guilty. She wished she could tell Clara about what had happened tonight. It would be nice to talk to someone who wasn't involved. Besides, it was awfully hard to keep such a big secret from her friend.

"Clara?" she whispered.

"Hmm?" Clara replied sleepily. "Something wrong?"

Mia sighed. She couldn't risk breaking a vow made on the power of the spell book. Not after what had happened tonight.

"No," she whispered. "Nothing's wrong."

"Hurry up, Mia, or we'll be late for class," Clara urged.

With a groan, Mia staggered out of bed and got dressed. She yawned so wide that her jaw cracked.

"You look like a raccoon with those dark circles under your eyes," Clara commented.

Mia yawned again. "I tossed and turned all night," she said, pulling her slippers on. "I'm ready now. Let's go."

They raced out into the hall. And Clara slammed into Alicia. Both girls tumbled to the floor.

Of all the bad luck, Mia thought as Clara scrambled to her feet. Some of the other students gathered a short distance away, watching.

"Are you all right?" Mia asked.

"I'm fine!" Alicia snapped. She started to get up, but got tangled in her silk skirts.

"Here, let me help you," Mia offered, holding out her hand.

Alicia slapped her hand away. "I don't need your help, farm girl!"

She climbed to her feet. Her face tightened with loathing as she turned to look at the girl who had bumped into her.

"Well, it's dear, sweet Clara Godert." Alicia sneered. "It seems that you're as clumsy as you are ugly. And everyone knows you're stupid, too. Even Miss Pemberthy thinks you're wasting your time here."

Clara's face went red, then white. Mia felt her own cheeks flush. She stepped in front of Clara. She had never been so angry in her life.

"You leave her alone, Alicia Bainbridge!" Mia cried.

The blond girl's eyes narrowed. "Who do you think you are?"

"You think that your daddy's money gives you the right to say or do anything to anyone," Mia retorted. "Well, I don't care about your daddy's money or your fancy clothes or your high-and-mighty airs. You're the cruelest, nastiest person I've ever met—"

"How dare you!"

Mia lifted her chin defiantly. "We've got a saying back home, that you can't make a silk purse out of a sow's ear. Well, you're a sow's ear right enough, Alicia Bainbridge. Mean and nasty and poor-spirited. All the silk gowns in the world aren't going to turn you into anything else."

Alicia's mouth opened and closed several times. But she didn't utter a word. Someone tittered.

Mia took Clara by the arm and urged her toward the stairs.

"I can't believe it," Clara murmured.

"What?" Mia asked, still furious.

"You won. You really won." A grin spread

over Clara's face. "I don't think that anyone has ever beaten Alicia in an argument before."

Mia laughed. "Well, it was long overdue."

They started downstairs. Joanna stood in the foyer, her coppery red hair gleaming in the morning light. She waved at Mia, then turned and went into the classroom.

"You sneaked out again last night," Clara told her. "I know you thought I was asleep, but I wasn't."

Mia studied the other girl for a moment, then sighed. "Yes, I did sneak out. Clara, I really wish I could tell you what's going on. But I made a very serious vow not to tell."

"Even me?" Clara asked.

"I'm sorry," Mia said helplessly.

"I'm really getting tired of doing dishes," Phoebe complained as they all walked toward the kitchen. "I don't think I've ever worked so hard in my life!"

Mia laughed. "You ought to live on a farm for a while. I'm used to getting up with the chickens and tending all the livestock before I even get to eat breakfast!"

"I'd rather die," Phoebe vowed.

"Me too," Joanna agreed.

Mia opened the door to the kitchen and gasped. She stopped so suddenly that Phoebe bumped into her.

Someone had splashed water over everything, then scattered the contents of a bag of flour. The mess had hardened into a paste on the floor . . . the walls . . . everything.

Mia gasped. Who could have done such a thing?

"Oh, no!" Phoebe wailed, peering over Mia's shoulder.

"What is it?" Joanna demanded. "Move, will you, so the rest of us can see!"

Mia and Phoebe stepped into the kitchen. Joanna, Irene, and Anabel filed in after them. Their faces filled with dismay as they looked around at the mess.

"I can't believe this," Anabel exclaimed.

"Oh, it's real," Joanna muttered.

Mia walked over to the table. The tablecloths and napkins they'd used at dinner last night were piled there.

She picked up one of the napkins and held it gingerly between her thumb and forefinger. The cloth was soaked with the flour paste. She dropped it, and it made a soft *splat* when it hit the floor.

"Disgusting!" Irene said.

"They put it on the tablecloths, too," Mia told them. "All the linens are going to have to be soaked, then scrubbed several times before they can be used again."

"This is going to take hours!" Irene wailed.

Joanna tapped her foot on the floor. "Miss Pemberthy isn't going to let us skip afternoon classes to do this. We'll have to wash them after dinner."

Mia spotted something on the floor nearby, and bent to pick it up. It was a yellow satin rosette—just like the ones adorning the expensive silk dress Alicia had on today.

"Look." She held it out to the others.

"Alicia!" they exclaimed in unison.

"This was her revenge for that argument we had," Mia told them. "I'm sorry that you have to suffer for it."

Phoebe tossed her head. "At least you told that snippy cat off. Ever since I came here, I've been wanting to see someone put her in her place."

Mia kicked at the napkin, sending it into a puddle of flour paste on the floor. "I wish I could make her dance the way that mouse did," she muttered. "I'd love to embarrass her in front of the whole school. It would serve her right!"

"What did you say?" Joanna demanded, her eyes suddenly bright.

"Huh? Oh, I said that I wish I could make Alicia dance like that mouse—"

"Yes!" Joanna cried. "It's perfect! Let's do it."

"You want to work a spell now? Here?" Mia asked in astonishment. "But we don't have the book of spells. How do you know it will even work?"

"Maybe we don't need the book," Joanna pointed out. "After all, we've practiced this spell over and over. Well, except for you, Mia. Do you remember it?"

"I think so," Mia told her.

Phoebe clapped her hands. "It's a wonderful idea."

Even Irene smiled. "Alicia is always so mean to everyone. She deserves it."

Mia looked around the kitchen again. Then she nodded. They wouldn't hurt Alicia, just humiliate her as she'd humiliated others. It was time she learned how it felt.

"Let's make the circle," Mia said. She

held out her hands to the other girls.

"Everyone think about Alicia while we chant," Joanna instructed. "Think about her dancing like the mouse."

They obeyed. Mia let the rhythm of the chant take her. The power came flooding through her. So quickly. Almost as if it had been waiting for her call.

A swirl of blue-white sparks flared to life in the air in the center of the circle.

The power gets stronger every time we use it, Mia thought.

The tiny, brilliant lights seemed to be dancing in time to the chant. They're beautiful, Mia thought.

The sparks shifted into a spiral. The spiral began to spin, slowly at first, then faster and faster, until Mia could see only a blur of light.

She pictured Alicia. And then she thought about the mouse dancing. *Twirling. Kicking its feet and twitching its whiskers.*

The spiral of sparks slowed. Now they formed the magical symbol from the spell book's cover.

Mia glanced at the others as they finished the chant. The blue-white light turned their faces into pale, eerie masks.

"Alicia," they murmured, their eyes glittering. "Alicia, Alicia, Alicia!"

Out in the schoolroom, someone screamed.

Chapter Nine

"That's Alicia!" Phoebe cried.

Mia whirled and raced out of the kitchen.

Had something awful happened? Had they gone too far and hurt Alicia somehow?

"Wait, Mia!" Joanna called after her, but Mia kept running.

As she neared the classroom, she heard the screams turn to laughter. Waves of laughter echoed through the school.

Mia rounded the corner and skidded to a stop in the doorway. Her mouth dropped open as she saw what was happening in the classroom.

Alicia was dancing. Her hair had fallen loose and hung in lank strands around her shoulders. Her face was red and sweaty. The fancy silk gown rustled madly as she spun and leaped.

"Ohh," Mia gasped.

Madame Guillaume, the French teacher, rapped her pointer on the desk. "Mademoiselle Bainbridge!" she cried. "You will stop this nonsense immediately!"

Alicia kept dancing. Mia knew she couldn't stop, no matter how much she wanted to.

Alicia's arms flopped awkwardly as she twirled and twirled. The other girls shrieked with laughter, even Alicia's followers.

"Alicia, Alicia!" Irene giggled. "Dance, Alicia!"

"Mademoiselle!" Madame Guillaume shrieked at the top of her lungs. "You will stop this at once, or I shall summon the headmistress!"

Terror filled Alicia's eyes as she leaped and spun, spun and leaped. Her breath came in harsh pants.

She was getting tired, Mia knew. But the

spell commanded her to dance, so she had to keep dancing.

Mia stared at Alicia. What if they couldn't stop the spell? What if Alicia danced on and on and on. Would she keep dancing until . . . until she died?

"No," Mia whispered. "Enough!"

The moment she spoke, she felt the power drain from her. The spell faded.

Alicia stopped dancing. She stood trembling, breathing in great, heaving gasps. Sweat poured down her face. A drop of it dangled from the end of her nose, quivering, then plopped to the floor.

That started the girls laughing even harder. Alicia's friends, the girls who had followed her and admired her and done everything she wanted, laughed and pointed with the rest.

Mia glanced at Joanna. Triumph glittered in the other girl's eyes. She was enjoying this, Mia knew.

"Alicia, don't you know that it is terribly unladylike to drip all over the floor?" Joanna taunted.

Alicia's lips trembled. Then she burst into tears and raced toward the door. She shoved Joanna aside, almost knocking her down.

Mia grabbed Joanna's arm and steadied her. Hate burned in Joanna's eyes as she watched Alicia run sobbing up the stairs.

"Girls, girls!" Madame Guillaume shouted. "Quiet now, all of you!"

Gradually, the laughter stopped. The teacher looked at Mia and the others. "You don't have your lesson papers, girls."

"They're upstairs, Madame Guillaume," Joanna told her. "We were in the kitchen doing the dishes, but we came running when we heard all the screaming."

"Well, go upstairs and fetch what you need," the teacher instructed, clapping her hands.

"But we haven't finished in the kitchen," Anabel protested.

"I will explain the situation to Miss Pemberthy," Madame Guillaume told them. "You may finish your chores after classes end for the day."

"Yes, Madame," Joanna replied.

She grabbed Mia's arm and dragged her back from the doorway. They hurried toward the stairs.

"That was wonderful!" Anabel whispered. "I've never seen anything so funny in my life!"

Phoebe giggled. "Did you see her face? Even her friends were laughing at her. She won't be lording over the rest of us again."

"No," Joanna agreed. Then her eyes narrowed. "I owe her for shoving me, though."

"I can't believe this," Irene crowed. "Dancing in the middle of the classroom like a madwoman! You were so clever to think of it, Mia!"

Mia nodded and smiled. But she didn't feel as happy as she'd thought she would. She didn't think she'd ever forget the misery in Alicia's eyes.

Mia felt her left hand begin to tingle. She opened it and stared down at her palm.

The symbol from the cover of the spell book was etched into her skin!

Chapter Ten

Mia stared down at her palm. The symbol looked as if it were burned into her flesh. But it didn't hurt.

She rubbed her hand on her skirt. Then she looked at her palm again. The symbol had disappeared.

"Is something the matter?" Joanna asked.

"Hold out your hands," Mia whispered.

They looked at her strangely, but did what she asked. None of them had a mark on their palms.

"What's wrong with you?" Joanna demanded.

"Nothing," Mia told her. "Nothing."

Why had she been the only one marked? What was happening to her?

"You're as skittish as my horse back home," Joanna complained. "Mia, you really have to get hold of yourself."

"Sometimes . . . sometimes I wonder if we should be doing any of this," Mia said.

Joanna pressed her lips into a tight line. Mia caught a glint of anger in her eyes. "We've already discussed this. It would be nice if someone could teach us exactly what to do. But that isn't going to happen. So we've got to just try spells and learn as we go along. Do you agree?"

"Well . . . yes," Mia admitted. Still, she couldn't help but remember that sick feeling in her stomach as she'd watched Alicia dance. "But—"

"It's really very simple, Mia," Joanna said. She crossed her arms over her chest. "We are going to do this. Either you're one of us, or you're not."

Mia didn't want to lose their friendship. And she would, if she didn't say yes. "Of course I'm one of you," she told them.

*   *   *

Mia stood by the window of the history classroom, waiting for the lesson to begin.

She stared outside and smiled. The whole world had turned white. It had been snowing all afternoon. And the thick white flakes continued to fall. She couldn't even see the barn from here.

That means there will be no meeting out there tonight, she thought. No spells. Good.

"I hope Goliath will be all right," Clara said from behind her.

Mia swung around to look at her roommate. "Don't worry about him. Cats know what to do. He'll be nice and cozy in the barn."

Clara nodded. She gazed out the window for a moment, then looked at Mia. "That was strange, what happened to Alicia. Don't you think?"

"I certainly do," Mia agreed. She hoped her face didn't give her away.

At that moment, Alicia sauntered into the room. She wore a blue silk gown that exactly matched her eyes. She also wore her usual haughty expression. Her followers came trooping in behind her.

She curled her lip disdainfully when she saw Mia and Clara. Putting her nose in the air, she stalked to her seat. The rustle of her silk skirts was loud in the quiet room.

"I guess you can only be but so embarrassed when your father is the richest man in the state," Clara whispered.

"I guess," Mia agreed.

A few at a time, the other students came in and took their seats. "We better sit down," Clara said. "Miss Pemberthy will be here any moment."

Mia took a deep breath and started for her chair. She sat across the aisle from Alicia. What bad luck!

"I hear your father raises pigs, farm girl," Alicia murmured as Mia passed her.

"Hogs," Mia corrected. Then she grimaced. She shouldn't have said anything at all. She'd only given Alicia something else to taunt her with.

"Oh, *hogs,*" Alicia echoed. "You must forgive my ignorance. I have had so little to do with . . . things like that. But I find it so fascinating." She smiled nastily. "Tell me, Mia . . . do hogs smell better than pigs?"

Joanna came in just in time to hear Alicia's question. She glared at Alicia.

"Yes," she replied before Mia could think of an answer. "And they have better manners than some people I know."

"Really?" Alicia drawled. "What would a shopkeeper's daughter know about manners?"

Joanna scowled. "You certainly are putting on a lot of airs for somebody who made a royal fool of herself today."

"That?" Alicia waved her hand carelessly. "I did that on purpose. I was just trying to liven things up a bit."

"You certainly did," one of her followers simpered. "I haven't laughed so hard in months. And old Madame Guillaume nearly had a fit!"

Triumph glinted in Alicia's eyes. She tilted her head back and stared at Joanna. "So, Miss Kershaw, who's the fool now?"

"Well . . . I'd nominate the person who thought that because something happened only once, it couldn't happen again," Joanna answered.

All the color drained from Alicia's cheeks.

Why did Joanna have to say that? Mia thought. She's just making Alicia suspicious.

"Exactly what do you mean?" Alicia demanded.

Joanna smiled. "You know exactly what I mean."

Miss Pemberthy bustled through the door, and Joanna took her seat.

Mia sighed with relief. She really, really didn't want Joanna to say any more.

"We're going to do something different for class today, girls," Miss Pemberthy told them. "I think it's time we studied some of the history of our very own village of Shadyside."

She rubbed her arms. "Goodness, it's chilly in here. That wind seems to be coming right through the walls today. Clara, you're closest to the fireplace. Would you add another log or two, please?"

Clara got up silently. She tossed two logs onto the fire and moved them into place with the poker. Miss Pemberthy pulled a chair over to the hearth. She gestured for the girls to sit in a half circle in front of her.

"There, that's cozy now," the headmistress said. "I don't suppose any of you think that there could be anything interesting about this quiet little village."

Mia shook her head.

"I thought not. But there can be interest in the simplest things, you know," Miss Pemberthy said. "This farmhouse was one of the first dwellings built here. Do you have any idea how long it's been standing?"

"Someone carved 1728 on one of the stones that hold up the front porch," one of the girls offered.

More than a hundred years ago, Mia thought in awe. It seemed like forever.

Miss Pemberthy inclined her head. "Yes. A man named Jacob Reade moved here from Salem, Massachusetts, that year. He built this house for his wife and young son."

"Miss Pemberthy?" Anabel called.

"Yes, Anabel?"

"Wasn't Salem where they had all the witch trials?" the girl asked.

"Yes, it was," Miss Pemberthy told them. "But of course, that was a very long time ago, and those people let superstition overcome their common sense. This is the nineteenth century. We know better about such things."

Mia glanced over at Joanna. Joanna winked at her.

Miss Pemberthy arranged her skirts daintily before continuing. "Why, there were people here in the village who said that Jacob's wife practiced the dark arts. That was a silly tale, of course, created by ignorant people simply because the Reades had come from Salem."

"But how do you know?" Alicia asked.

"Know what, dear?"

"How do you know that Jacob's wife didn't practice the dark arts?" Alicia persisted.

Miss Pemberthy smiled fondly at her favorite student. "Because there is no such thing as the dark arts," she replied. "Now, let's go on to Shadyside proper, which was founded in—"

Mia's thoughts wandered away from the lesson. So, people had claimed Jacob Reade's wife practiced the dark arts. And she'd lived right here in this house.

Where Joanna had found the spell book.

A coldness crept through Mia, and it had nothing to do with the snowstorm outside. She raised her hand.

Miss Pemberthy looked over at her. "Yes, Miss Saxton?"

"What did people say Mrs. Reade did . . ." Mia paused for a moment, then went on with a rush. "Did they say she did good things or bad things with her power?"

"Miss Saxton, we've already moved on to another part of the lesson," Miss Pemberthy chided gently. "Apparently, however, you didn't move with us."

Mia ducked her head to hide her flaming cheeks. "I'm sorry, Ma'am."

"Well, all right." The headmistress folded her hands on her knee. "To answer your question," she continued, "Emma Reade had no powers, good or bad. Such powers do not exist. Is that clear?"

"Yes, Ma'am," Mia replied. She wondered if Miss Pemberthy would have been so sure if she'd felt the power just once!

The headmistress went on with the lesson. Mia shot another glance at Joanna. The other girl shook her head slightly. Keep quiet, her expression said. Don't ask any more questions.

Mia knew she was right. But nothing was going to keep her from asking the questions of herself. And wondering.

The power existed. It was real. Mia had touched it, felt it. Used it.

Had Emma Reade used it, too?

Had she written her spells into that book

and left it so that someone else could use it?

And if she had . . . why?

Mia looked up, and saw that Alicia was staring at Joanna. Suspicion glinted in the blond girl's eyes.

Then Alica turned her gaze on Mia. She knows, Mia thought. She knows!

Chapter Eleven

Ｓhe's going to say something, Mia thought. Any moment now, and she's just going to burst out with it! She's going to announce to everyone that we are practicing the dark arts.

Mia was scared. Of all the people who might discover their secret, Alicia was the worst.

Alicia continued to stare at Joanna. Then she opened her mouth wide—and screamed.

Mia felt her chest tighten. What was Alicia doing?

"A spider!" Alicia shrieked, pointing to Joanna's skirt.

Relief swept through Mia. A spider. She was screaming about a little spider!

Miss Pemberthy leaped to her feet. "Alicia Bainbridge, you scared me nearly to death!"

Joanna reached over and flicked off the spider. "It's only a tiny little spider, Alicia. It wasn't going to hurt me or you."

"I hate spiders!" Alicia cried. "Hate them, hate them, hate them!"

She grabbed a book and slammed it down, smashing the spider. "Ugh! Disgusting creature," she panted.

Clara leaned close to Mia. "I guess spiders don't go into rich people's homes," she whispered.

Mia tried not to laugh. She didn't want Miss Pemberthy to scold her.

Miss Pemberthy started to talk again. Mia struggled to put everything out of her head and concentrate on the lesson. But she found it nearly impossible. She kept worrying about what would happen if Alicia found out about them.

She had to talk to the others. She had to warn them to be especially careful around Alicia.

"Well, girls," the headmistress finally

said. "You may be excused. And don't be late for your drawing class."

Thank goodness! Mia thought. She had to talk to the others before Joanna said another word to Alicia!

But Joanna and the others were closer to the door, and went out before Mia could get their attention. Mia hurried after them.

Out of the corner of her eye she saw Clara coming toward her. Oh, no! she thought. She couldn't stop to talk to Clara now.

Mia grabbed her papers and hurried out of the room. She pretended she hadn't seen Clara. She had to catch up with the others.

"Joanna!" Mia called. "Wait!"

Joanna turned. Anabel, Phoebe, and Irene turned with her. Mia rushed up to them. She glanced over her shoulder to make sure no one was watching them before speaking.

"I think Alicia suspects that someone put a spell on her," she whispered.

"Why do you think that?" Joanna asked.

"No matter what she told other people, *she* knows that she didn't mean to dance like that," Mia told them. "Then you said it could happen again, and just a few minutes later Miss Pemberthy told that story about Emma Reade practicing the dark arts—"

"Shhhh," Joanna whispered. "We had better not talk about it here. We'll meet in my room tonight. All of us."

The hall clock had chimed midnight by the time Mia reached Joanna's room. Irene, Phoebe, and Anabel were already there.

"What took you so long?" Joanna demanded.

"Clara didn't fall asleep until a little while ago," Mia explained. "Remember, I'm the only one rooming with someone who isn't part of the group. If Clara could join—"

"No," Anabel snapped. "Not her. She's too, uh . . ."

"Odd," Irene supplied.

"No, she's nice," Mia protested. "If you would only try and talk to her—"

"We've got more important things to discuss," Joanna interrupted. "Like what we're going to do about Alicia."

"Let's put another spell on her," Anabel suggested eagerly.

"Yes, yes!" Phoebe seconded. "Let's make her do something so ridiculous that she'll have to leave school."

Mia didn't want to do any more spells on people. But they did have to find some way to make sure Alicia didn't find out their secret.

Joanna shook her head. "If something peculiar like that happens again, Miss Pemberthy is bound to start asking questions. You know Alicia is her pet."

The others nodded. Mia nodded, too.

"So the best thing to do," Joanna continued, "is to be very quiet and careful. Alicia doesn't have proof of anything. And after all, she can't very well tattle that she thinks we're doing spells. Even Miss Pemberthy isn't going to believe that."

"You have to admit that it was a lot of fun to make her dance, though," Anabel said with a giggle.

Now that it was all over, Mia had to admit that it *had* been awfully funny. Alicia hadn't been hurt, only embarrassed. Besides, she'd been so mean that it was hard to feel sorry for her.

"Let's try another spell," Joanna suggested.

"Here?" Phoebe demanded.

"As long as we're quiet, no one will know," Joanna said. "Remember, we cast that spell on Alicia without using the book or the symbol. I think it's important that we try again to see if we can do it whenever we want."

Joanna got the book out of its hiding place in her bureau drawer. "I found one of the simpler spells. We can memorize it in just a few minutes."

She set the book down on her bed, gesturing for them all to gather around her. It was an easy spell. Mia had it memorized after two readings. Then she reached out and touched the brittle page.

"It's very old," she said. "I wonder if it really was Emma Reade's spell book."

"It doesn't matter," Joanna told her. "We found it. It belongs to us now."

Mia nodded. But one tiny corner of her mind wondered if they had found it . . . or if it had found them.

"Is everyone ready?" Joanna asked. She left the book sitting open on the bed. Then she blew out the lamp, leaving the room lit only by a single candle.

She set the candlestick on the floor. The girls took their places around it. They began to chant in a whisper.

Mia's palm tingled. She glanced down at

it. The symbol was beginning to form there on her skin. It grew clearer with every word of the chant.

Something strange was happening to her.

The chant echoed in her ears as if a hundred people were whispering it along with her. She could hear her own heartbeat. She could even hear all the heartbeats around her.

Power spurted along her veins. Strong, so strong.

Something pulled her gaze to the bed. To the spell book. A page lifted. Turned. Another page stirred. Turned.

Mia felt a change in the air. The tingling in her hand was so strong now that it almost hurt.

Another page turned. Another. The pages began to flip swiftly, almost as though a breeze had caught them.

But there isn't a breeze, Mia thought.

Mia looked down at the candle flame. It didn't waver at all.

The yellow flame burned steadily, without a flicker.

Then the flame grew darker. Becoming a deep orange.

Mia began to feel sleepy.

Then the flame grew darker still. It glowed a rich brown.

Mia's tongue felt thick as she continued to chant. It was such an effort to speak each word.

And the flame continued to change. Growing even darker. Turning black.

Chapter Twelve

Mia watched the black flame flicker and dance. It threw an eerie purple light into the room.

She stared at the other girls. The strange light transformed their faces. They all look like fiends, she thought. I must look like a fiend, too.

Does a dark flame mean the spell is dark? Mia wondered.

She felt her arms break out in gooseflesh. Should they stop the spell?

Knock. Knock.

Mia stopped chanting.

"Someone's at the door," Anabel whispered.

"Shhhh. Don't answer it yet!" Joanna ordered. She jumped to her feet. "Mia, hurry and put the candle out!"

Mia tried to lift her hand, but her muscles wouldn't obey her. It was as if the black flame had put her under a spell.

Her body felt so heavy. And she felt so, so tired.

Phoebe blew the candle out. Joanna snatched the book off the sheets and shoved it under the bed.

Mia suddenly felt wide awake and alert. What were they going to do? What explanation could they give for being up at this hour?

Knock! Knock! Knock!

"Joanna Kershaw, you open this door immediately!" Miss Pemberthy cried.

"Oh, no!" Irene whispered.

Joanna heaved a sigh. "We're caught. Phoebe, you might as well light the lamp."

Mia heard the *scritch* of a match being lit, then light blossomed in the room. Irene looked pale and scared.

"Joanna!" Miss Pemberthy rapped sharply on the door again. "Please don't keep me waiting."

"I'm coming," Joanna called. She swung open the door.

Miss Pemberthy strode into the room. Her mouth was set in a thin, tight line. Her eyes glittered with annoyance.

Alicia followed her into the room. "I told you something strange was going on in here!" Alicia cried.

Miss Pemberthy's eyebrows rose. "I see nothing strange. Just five disobedient girls."

"But I heard them chanting," Alicia insisted. "It wasn't even English!"

"Indeed." The headmistress crossed her arms over her chest and regarded Mia and the others. "Would any of you care to offer an explanation?"

Mia's mind went blank, leaving her speechless.

But Joanna answered quickly. "We weren't chanting, Miss Pemberthy," she explained. "We were singing. It was that song Madame Guillaume taught us . . . uh, '*Frère Jacques*.'"

Mia felt her mouth drop open. It was a very good lie. And Joanna even managed an expression of complete innocence when she told it!

"That's a lie!" Alicia cried. "Miss Pemberthy, she's lying! They were chanting. I think they are practicing—"

"Alicia." Miss Pemberthy's tone was sharp. "I've heard about enough for one evening. It's late. Run along to bed, now."

Alicia shot Joanna a hate-filled glance. "Yes, Miss Pemberthy."

Alicia flounced off down the hall. Miss Pemberthy fixed Mia and her friends with a stern gaze. "Now, ladies, you know when you are expected to be in bed. Is there some reason why you girls feel that the rules do not apply to you?"

They all shook their heads. Miss Pemberthy stared at each one of them in turn. Mia couldn't look her in the eye. She hated lying, even if they'd had no choice.

"I can't hear you," the headmistress snapped.

Mia ducked her head. "We were wrong, Ma'am. We know it."

"Well!" Miss Pemberthy let her breath out in a sigh. "At least you admit it. But that won't keep you from washing dishes again tomorrow."

"Yes, ma'am," they chorused.

Miss Pemberthy turned abruptly and left.

"Phew!" Phoebe breathed. "I don't mind an extra day of dishes—as long as she doesn't tell my parents!"

"I think Alicia was about to tell Miss Pemberthy that we were practicing the dark arts," Mia exclaimed.

"Don't worry," Joanna said. "She's only guessing. She—"

Mia heard footsteps rushing down the hall. Then Alicia burst back into the room.

"You're up to something very strange," Alicia accused. "And I'm going to find out what it is. When I do, none of you will be attending *this* school anymore."

"You shouldn't make threats unless you know what you're up against," Joanna told her.

I wish Joanna hadn't said that, Mia thought. Alicia is suspicious enough as it is.

"I'm not afraid of you, Joanna Kershaw!" Alicia retorted.

Joanna leaned forward, pushing her face close to Alicia's. "Maybe you should be," she said, her voice low.

"Stop it," Mia whispered. She stepped between the two girls. "Joanna, stop it."

Alicia turned and stalked away. She paused in the doorway and glared at them over her shoulder. "Remember," she called. "I'm going to find out exactly what nastiness you all are up to. And when I do, you'll be finished!"

She left, slamming the door behind her. Mia gave a sigh of relief that things hadn't been any worse.

Then she saw the candle. The black flame had sprung to life again. It fluttered and cast that strange purple light.

"Who lit the candle?" she asked.

But she already knew the answer. None of them had lit it.

"It lit itself," Irene whispered.

Mia's hand began to tingle. The tingle grew deeper, sharper. With a soft cry of alarm, Mia held her hand up in front of her face.

Her palm was on fire.

Chapter Thirteen

Mia was afraid to move, afraid to
do anything that might make the flame
spread.

Then she realized it didn't hurt.

"Grab the sheet and wrap it around her
hand," Joanna ordered.

"Wait," Mia said. "It's not burning me."

Phoebe's eyes grew round as she stared
at Mia's hand. A low moan escaped from
Irene's throat.

How could this be? Mia thought. Fire

burned. But this fire, this black fire, didn't burn her skin.

She turned her palm over so that it faced the floor. The black flame didn't curl upward like a normal flame. No. It just burned downward, as if the floor had become the ceiling.

Mia began to feel sleepy again. Her arms and legs felt heavy. It wasn't an unpleasant sensation, just strange.

Anabel clutched Mia's shoulder. "Are you sure it's not hurting you?" she asked. Her voice sounded higher than usual.

Mia nodded. "I'm fine."

Slowly, Mia turned her palm upright, bringing the black flame with it.

"Mia, put it out!" Irene gasped.

"Don't worry," Mia assured her. "It just tickles a little."

"But we don't know what it's doing to you," Irene said.

"You're such a litle goose," Joanna snapped.

"What is it?" Phoebe asked. "It's just like the flame that appeared when we were chanting."

Anabel ran to the dresser. Gingerly, she reached out toward the black candle flame.

"Don't touch it!" Irene begged.

Anabel started to snatch her hand back. But the black flame leaped to her hand.

She cried out. Then she smiled in delight.

"It really *doesn't* burn," she told the others.

"Are you sure?" Irene asked doubtfully.

"Of course I'm sure," Anabel retorted. "Do you think I would stand here and let it burn me?"

After a moment, Phoebe held her hand out. "Let me try," she said.

Anabel reached toward her. The flame jumped to Phoebe's hand. She laughed. "It does tickle."

Joanna held her hand out in front of Mia. Mia poured her flame into the other girl's palm.

"It's so pretty," Joanna murmured, holding it up to her face. "You try it, Irene."

Irene started to back up, but Joanna was too quick. She transferred the flame to Irene's hand.

"I wonder what it's supposed to do," Joanna said.

"I don't know. I . . ." Mia's voice trailed off as she noticed the change in Joanna's face. A red glow shone from her pupils, as though a bonfire burned behind her eyes.

She glanced at the other girls. Their eyes glowed red too.

Mia's breath caught in her throat. Suddenly she didn't think the flames were quite so nice anymore.

"What's wrong, Mia?" Joanna asked, her voice dreamy, faraway.

"I think we'd better stop," Mia said.

Instantly, all the flames vanished.

"Why did you do that?" Joanna demanded angrily. The red glow had left her eyes.

Mia quickly checked the other girls. Their eyes had returned to normal. We're all unharmed, she reassured herself.

"Mia, why did you make the flames go out?" Joanna repeated.

"I didn't do anything," Mia protested. "I only said we ought to stop. Miss Pemberthy's going to come back—"

"And we're going to be in the worst trouble of our lives," Irene finished for her.

Joanna nodded. "You'd all better return to your rooms. Tomorrow night, though, plan to meet in the barn. Alicia is not going to stop us. If we have to, we'll stop her first."

Mia stared intently at Joanna. How seri-

FEAR STREET SAGAS®

Please check:

1. How many books have you read in the *Fear Street Sagas* series?
☐ 0 ☐ 1-3 ☐ 4-6 ☐ 7-10

2. How much did you like this *Fear Street Sagas* book, CIRCLE OF FIRE?
☐ loved it ☐ liked it ☐ it was okay ☐ did not like it ☐ hated it

3. Please rank in order of importance the following (#1 being best):
☐ Horror ☐ Romance ☐ Suspense ☐ History ☐ Fear Family Curse

4. How did you first hear of CIRCLE OF FIRE?
☐ advertisement ☐ from a friend ☐ in school ☐ in a store display
☐ On-line (site address:) _____
☐ other _____

5. Would you buy another *Fear Street Sagas* book?
☐ definitely ☐ most likely ☐ maybe ☐ probably not ☐ no

6. Which would you prefer to find in a *Fear Street Sagas* book
(please rank, #1 being best)? _____ coupon (SSS off your next book)
_____ bookmark _____ sweepstakes entry _____ tattoos _____ stickers
_____ letter from R.L. Stine _____ nothing _____ Fear Family Tree
other _____

7. What other series books do you read?
☐ Fear Street Sagas® ☐ Ghosts of Fear Street® ☐ Goosebumps® ☐ Sabrina
☐ Dean Koontz ☐ Sweet Valley High ☐ V.C. Andrews ☐ Stephen King
☐ other _____

YOUR OPINION COUNTS!
Just complete and drop into any mailbox— no postage necessary!

8. What magazines do you read? ☐ Nickelodeon ☐ Disney Adventures
☐ Seventeen ☐ Mad Magazine ☐ Rolling Stone ☐ Teen Beat
☐ People ☐ American Girl ☐ Teen ☐ Sports Illustrated ☐ YM
☐ other _____

9. How often do you go on the internet? ☐ once a day ☐ once a week
☐ once a month ☐ never

10. Are you ☐ Male ☐ Female?

Your name: _____

Date of Birth: _____ / _____ / _____

Street Address: _____

City, _____

State, Zip code: _____

Thank you for participating!

© 1998 by Parachute Press, Inc. FEAR STREET SAGAS is a registered trademark of Parachute Press, Inc.
Gold Key®'s is trademark of Golden Books Publishing Company, Inc.

ous was she? she wondered. How far would she really go to stop Alicia?

"Which spell are we going to do?" Phoebe asked when they met in the barn the next night.

"Let's do the same one we did last night," Anabel suggested. "Maybe we can get all the candle flames to turn black."

"I don't think—" Mia began.

"I have another idea," Joanna told them.

She gestured for them to sit. They made the circle, the firelight flickering all around them. Joanna opened the book and set it on the floor.

"The candle spell was marked with a star," she said, tapping the open page. "And so is this one. Maybe they're the same kind of spell."

"Are we going to use the book and the symbol tonight?" Anabel asked.

"I've been thinking about that," Joanna admitted. "Last night, we did the spell without them. But remember, the flame only appeared on Mia's hand. I wonder if the spell was weaker because we didn't use the book and symbol."

"I'd rather use them, then," Anabel said.

Joanna nodded. Then she looked over at Mia, and gave her a mocking sort of smile. "You are the one who's always worrying about danger, Mia. Well, you and Irene. But she doesn't count. She's afraid of everything."

Irene gave a little squeak of protest, and Joanna laughed.

"What do you think, Mia?" Joanna asked.

Mia didn't dare say what she really thought. Joanna wouldn't like it. And if Joanna didn't like it, the others wouldn't, either.

"I'll do what everyone else does," she told them.

"Good," Joanna murmured. "Irene? Phoebe?"

"Use the book and symbol," Phoebe voted.

Irene hesitated for a moment. Then she nodded. "Use them," she said.

Joanna handed Mia a piece of charcoal. "It's your turn to draw the symbol."

Mia took the charcoal and began to draw. Her hand moved quickly, without hesitation.

"How did you remember it?" Anabel asked.

"I always have to study the book cover," Phoebe added.

"I have a good memory," Mia replied.

But somehow it didn't feel as if she were remembering the symbol. It was more as if she had known it forever. As if there had never been a time she wasn't familiar with every line, every detail.

Mia finished the symbol and set down the charcoal.

"Let's start," Joanna said. They joined hands and began to chant.

Mia felt the power rise in the room. In her. The candle flames dimmed and began to die.

Shadows gathered close and thick. Mia knew she ought to be afraid. But she was caught up in the chant. In the power.

The rhythm pulsed through her with every beat of her heart. She had no choice but to keep going.

Tiny, blue-white flames sprang up along the outlines of the charcoal symbol.

Mia stared at the leaping flames, entranced.

Then the flames grew darker—and turned black.

She felt a great rushing in her ears, but

there was no wind. None of the others seemed to hear it.

This spell is strong. Stronger than the one last night. Stronger and somehow darker.

It is evil, Mia realized.

Mia felt as if her ribs were being pushed together. Her lungs began to burn.

She couldn't breathe.

But she kept chanting. Her lips seemed to move on their own.

She glanced down at her palm. The symbol had formed, darker than ever.

Red dots exploded in front of Mia's eyes.

She had to stop it! Now!

Too late.

The spell was finished.

Mia pulled in a huge breath of air. I was suffocating, she thought.

"Nothing happened," Joanna said. "The spell didn't work!"

Mia stared at her. "Can't you feel it?" she demanded. "Can't any of you feel it?"

"What?" Irene whispered.

"I don't know exactly what happened," Mia answered. "But I know the spell worked."

I have to look outside, Mia thought. I have to find out what we've done.

She pushed herself to her feet. Her legs trembled as she crossed to the window. She stared out into the night.

Wind-driven snow swirled along the ground. The whole world looked as though it had been covered with a blanket of pure white.

Pure except for that dark patch on the ground near the oak tree, Mia thought. What is it?

She wiped off the window with her sleeve and peered out again. But she still couldn't see what was out there.

Mia slowly walked out of the barn. She could hear the others following.

Mia headed toward the dark spot on the snow. The feeling of *wrongness* worsened the nearer she got.

She wanted to turn and run. She wanted to run straight upstairs and climb into bed.

But she couldn't. She had to see. She had to know.

Mia took three steps closer and stopped. The dark spot . . . it was moving.

Mia forced herself to take one more step. She leaned down and stared at the dark spot.

Spiders.

A living carpet of them, crawling, squirming, running across one another's backs. Thousands of them.

Mia backed away. She bumped into Joanna.

"What did we do?" Mia whispered.

"It's just some spiders," Joanna answered. "They are more afraid of us than we are of—"

Irene sank to the ground. She sat in the snow, shivering.

"What is the matter with you?" Joanna demanded.

"There's someone . . . there's someone," Irene stammered. She pointed to the spiders.

An arm. An arm was sticking out of the swarm of spiders.

Mia felt a sharp taste hit the back of her throat.

"There's someone underneath them," Irene choked out.

Chapter Fourteen

Mia bent down and grabbed a fistful of snow. She hurled it at the spiders.

They moved off into the woods in a black wave.

"Noooo," Mia wailed.

Alicia stared up at her. Stared up at her with blank, unseeing eyes.

Her blue lips gaped open in a silent scream.

Mia squeezed her eyes shut. Please don't let her be dead, she prayed.

She opened her eyes. She moved next to Alicia and knelt beside her. She gently touched Alicia's arm.

Alicia did not move.

Mia shook Alicia's arm. "Get up," she cried. "Alicia, get up."

"She's dead," Joanna said. "Look at her, Mia. She's dead. There's nothing you can do for her."

Mia stared into Alicia's face. Then she reached out and pressed Alicia's eyelids closed.

"Come on," Phoebe said. "We have to go get Miss Pemberthy."

Mia didn't want to leave Alicia. She knew Alicia was dead. But she didn't want to leave her alone out in the snow.

"I'm going to get her," Phoebe said.

Mia started to stand. She saw something move in the dark cave of Alicia's mouth. Move and wiggle.

She let out a soft cry of horror as two long, hairy legs emerged from Alicia's open mouth. They felt around, touching, tapping.

A spider. The biggest spider Mia had ever seen was crawling out of Alicia's mouth.

nabel shrieked as the huge spider squeezed its way out of Alicia's mouth. It scurried across her cheek and then darted across the snow into the woods.

Alicia is dead because of what we did, Mia thought. Because we had to use the power.

She felt tears sting her eyes. She brushed them away with the back of her hand.

Mia heard a shout behind her. She dragged her gaze from Alicia and saw Miss Pemberthy running toward her. The headmistress hadn't even bothered to put on her robe.

Irene scrambled up and threw herself at Miss Pemberthy. "She's dead. She's dead," Irene wailed.

"Did any of you see what happened?" Miss Pemberthy asked.

"No, Miss Pemberthy," Joanna said. "We heard a noise and found her like this."

"Go back to your rooms, all of you," Miss Pemberthy said gently. "I'll handle this."

Mia heard the other girls start back toward the school. But she couldn't move.

"Get up, Mia," Miss Pemberthy said softly.

Mia felt frozen. She couldn't stop staring at Alicia.

The headmistress rushed over and pulled her away from the hideous sight.

"Oh, Alicia!" Miss Pemberthy cried. "Did you see anything, Mia? Do you know what happened to Alicia?"

We killed her, Mia thought. We did it with the spell.

"No, we found her like this," Mia answered. Her voice sounded flat and lifeless.

Miss Pemberthy took her by the arms and shook her gently.

"Mia, you must go back to the house. Tell Miss Connors to send Timothy for the doctor." She gave Mia another shake. "Can you hear me?"

Mia blinked. Then she nodded. "Yes, Ma'am."

Miss Pemberthy pushed her gently toward the house. Mia started out at a walk. But once she got her feet going, they moved faster and faster, until she was running.

She gave Miss Pemberthy's message to Miss Connors. Everyone was awake, although the girls had been ordered to stay in their rooms.

Mia felt sure that anyone who looked at her would be able to see that she was guilty. But no one seemed to notice. Miss Connors sent her to her room.

Mia ran upstairs, glad to escape. She raced down the hall as fast as she could. She burst into the room and slammed the door behind her.

"What's the matter?" Clara asked. "We heard screams. Has something happened?"

Yes, Mia thought. Something's happened. Alicia is dead. And we killed her.

"Alicia . . . We found her outside, under

the big oak tree . . ." Mia had to take a deep breath to keep going. "She's dead."

"Dead!" Clara exclaimed. "Oh, no!"

Mia nodded. Then she curled up on her bed and wrapped her arms around herself.

"Never again," she whispered under her breath. "Never, never, never!"

Clara sat down beside her. "It will be all right, Mia," she murmured, patting her on the shoulder.

Mia couldn't bear being comforted. Not after what they had done. "It won't be all right!" she cried. "Nothing will ever be all right again."

She leaped off the bed and ran from the room. Clara called after her, but Mia kept running. She had to be alone, if only for a few minutes!

The door to the attic stood ajar, and Mia slipped through. She hurried up the stairs and sank down on the floor. Her tears made dark splotches in the dust.

She tried to forget Alicia's dead face. She tried to forget the spider squeezing out of her mouth.

But she couldn't. Maybe she never would.

"Mia!" someone whispered.

"Go away," she answered.

Footsteps approached her. She turned to see Joanna and the others. Anabel and Irene were crying. Phoebe seemed calm, but her eyes held a haunted, horrified expression.

Joanna let out a long sigh. "We have to talk. We have to figure out what to do about this."

Mia rubbed the tears from her cheeks. Anabel found a blanket among the storage boxes and spread it on the floor. The girls gathered around Mia, clinging to one another.

After a moment, Joanna pulled away. "What did you tell Miss Pemberthy, Mia?"

"Just that we found Alicia dead," Mia answered.

"Good," Joanna said. "That's what we told them, too. And everyone is so upset about Alicia being dead that they don't seem to care that we were outside without permission again."

"Tell her," Anabel said quietly.

Joanna nodded. "Mia, the rest of us have sworn not to tell what really happened tonight. We want you to swear, too."

"How could I tell anyone?" Mia asked.

"Would Miss Pemberthy believe me if I told her we did a spell that caused hundreds of spiders to attack Alicia?"

"We want you to promise," Anabel told her. "We have to be sure you won't tell."

Mia looked at each of them. "All right. I promise."

"Swear," Joanna commanded.

Joanna pulled the spell book out from beneath her robe. Mia swallowed hard. She didn't want to touch that ever again.

"Swear!" Joanna snapped.

Mia rested her hand on the spell book. The cover felt warm under her palm. Almost as if it were alive, she thought.

Mia closed her eyes. "I swear," she whispered. "I will not tell what happened to Alicia—"

"Or the power will punish you," Joanna finished for her.

"Or the power will punish me," Mia echoed.

Joanna took the book back and tucked it under her robe.

"No one will ever find out. We're safe," Irene said.

"They have too many other things to think about now," Phoebe agreed.

Mia couldn't believe it. "Even if we never get caught, we know the truth," she cried. "Alicia is dead because of our spell!"

"We didn't mean for it to happen," Phoebe protested.

"Alicia was snooping," Anabel pointed out. "Maybe if she'd minded her own business, that wouldn't have happened to her."

"And maybe not," Mia argued. "Maybe the spell chose her because we all hated her."

"It wasn't our fault!" Irene cried.

Mia clenched her fists. "It was our fault. We played with the power and it killed Alicia."

"It doesn't matter, anyway," Joanna said, tossing her head. "No one liked Alicia. She was mean and cruel. She deserved it."

Mia's stomach twisted as she looked at them. They didn't even feel guilty about it!

They loved the power. They thought it gave them the right to do anything to anyone.

And they would keep doing spells until someone else got hurt. Or killed.

Mia knew what she had to do.

"I'm quitting," she told them. "No more spells."

"What?" Joanna gasped.

Mia crossed her arms over her chest. "I've sworn not to tell anyone that we are responsible for what happened to Alicia. But I'm not going to have anything to do with that power again."

"But we need you," Phoebe protested.

Mia shook her head. "At first, I was curious, just like you. I wanted to find out what the power would do. Now we know. It's dangerous. And I'm not working any more spells. Ever."

"Mia, please," Anabel begged. "The spell book said five girls are needed to complete the circle."

"And think about what we can do once we learn more," Joanna added. "When we learn how to properly control the power—"

"Don't you hear yourselves?" Mia cried. "Didn't you see what happened to Alicia? You're mad if you think you're ever going to control *that*."

Joanna's expression grew cold. She stood. The others stared at her.

Phoebe rose and stood next to Joanna. Then Anabel joined them.

Irene looked from Mia to Joanna.

Irene won't go with them, Mia thought.

She knows how dangerous the spells are. She was afraid of them from the beginning.

Irene rose, and stood beside Phoebe.

They all stared down at Mia.

"You don't want to be our friend," Joanna said.

"I can't work another spell," Mia answered. "I can't risk killing again."

"You'll be sorry," Joanna promised.

Chapter Sixteen

Mia walked through the woods behind the schoolhouse. Stars filled the sky. The trees stood like dark pillars against the snow.

She heard the faraway sound of singing. No, not singing. Chanting.

Alicia hasn't been dead one whole day, and they are already trying another spell.

What will it do this time?

Alarm sent icy daggers spearing through

her. It wasn't good to be out here alone with the chanting. Even as she thought that, the voices grew louder.

"Mia, Mia, Mia."

They are chanting my name, she realized.

Joanna said I would be sorry. Are they doing a spell to hurt me?

To kill me?

Mia turned and ran back toward the schoolhouse. The snow squeaked beneath her feet.

The voices grew louder. Louder. Time was running out.

She tried to run faster. But her feet felt so heavy. So slow.

It's the spell, she thought. The spell is holding me back.

Her breath burned in her chest as she struggled forward. She could feel danger. It was coming. And if she didn't run fast enough, it would catch her.

She glanced behind her. A dark spot moved across the forest floor. Dark and squirming, a living carpet that flowed across the snow toward her.

Spiders.

Alicia hadn't been enough. They were still hungry, and they were coming for her.

Scream, Mia ordered herself. Call for help.

She opened her mouth to shriek—but no sound came out.

Her steps grew slower.

She turned and looked behind her. The spiders were closer now.

And the rhythm of the chant seemed to fill the woods, the whole world. "Mia, Mia, Mia."

Mia tried to move forward. She had to reach the school.

But the chant swirled around her, and she couldn't get her body to obey. She was rooted in place, planted deep like the trees around her.

The spiders were so close now that she could hear the skitter of their legs on the snow. It wouldn't be long before they were on her.

And then she'd be dead. Dead just like Alicia.

She watched them come.

Someone began to laugh. It was a terrible laugh, full of malice and evil. Joanna.

"I told you," Joanna cried. "I told you that you'd be sorry!"

The first spider reached Mia's feet. It began to climb up her skirt.

It moved quickly. It scurried over the buttons of her blouse. Then up her neck, over her chin—and into her mouth.

"Noooooooooo!"

Mia sat up with a gasp. She was in her bed, in her room.

Clara was asleep in the bed across from hers. Mia could hear her deep, quiet breathing.

Mia closed her eyes with a sigh. It was a dream! Only a dream.

"Only a dream," she whispered under her breath.

Out of the corner of her eye, she caught a glimpse of movement on her bed. She peered down at the quilt that covered her legs.

Her breath went out in a *whoosh*. Her heart seemed to stop. Then it gave a hard thump and began to pound.

A spider. A spider as big as her fist.

It had come for her.

Chapter Seventeen

Mia screamed.

With a startled cry, Clara leaped out of bed. "Mia, what is it?" she exclaimed.

"Get it off me!" Mia shrieked. "The spider! Get it away from me!"

Clara gasped when she saw the size of the spider on Mia's quilt. Then she leaned closer.

"Be careful," Mia begged.

"It's just a shadow," Clara told her. She ran her hand over Mia's covers. "See, it's just a shadow."

Clara glanced around the room. "The real spider is over there on the window. It's tiny. It's nothing to be afraid of."

Mia let out a sigh of relief. The bright moonlight made the small spider's shadow enormous.

"I was dreaming about spiders," she murmured. "They were chasing me through the woods and . . ." Taking a deep breath, she tried to get control of her trembling. "It seemed so real. And then I woke up and saw that shadow."

Clara nodded. "I'm not surprised you had a bad dream tonight. Not after you found Alicia." She sat down on the edge of Mia's bed. "Could you tell . . . how she died?"

Spiders came out of her mouth, Mia thought. From inside her.

"Uh . . . no," Mia answered. "She was just lying there when I found her."

"Oh." Clara got to her feet. "Well, poor Alicia."

Mia lifted her head in surprise. "You feel sorry for her, even after how she treated you?"

Clara shrugged. "I didn't like her, of course. But that doesn't mean I'm glad she died."

Remembering how heartless Joanna and the others had been, Mia had to swallow hard to keep from crying. Clara was a better person than the whole selfish group of them!

"Thanks for helping me, Clara," she said. "You're a true friend."

"I know," Clara replied.

Clara had already gone when Mia woke the next morning. Mia dressed quickly and ran downstairs. She followed the smell of ham and fresh-baked biscuits to the dining room.

As she neared the doorway, she heard Joanna laugh. And suddenly, Mia wasn't hungry anymore. She didn't want to be around any of them. Especially Joanna.

Mia turned away. As she walked past the parlor, a faint perfume caught her attention. Roses!

Now, where would they get roses in midwinter? she wondered. Then she nodded. Old Mr. Hazelton down the road kept a hothouse behind his house.

The parlor door was closed. Mia turned the latch and found it unlocked. Drawn by the sweet perfume, she stepped inside.

"Oh!" she gasped.

Alicia's coffin sat on a low table in the center of the room. Miss Pemberthy must have decided to lay out her body here, until her parents come to claim it, Mia thought.

The coffin was open. But the lid hid Mia's view of Alicia's body.

Mia wanted to turn and run out of the room. But she forced herself to stay where she was.

She had done this to Alicia. At least she'd helped make this happen. And she had something to say to the girl who lay in that wooden box.

Slowly, reluctantly, she walked toward the coffin.

The scent of the roses grew stronger. Sweet, so sweet.

Mia could see the dead girl now. She looked peaceful, almost as though she'd fallen asleep. No one would have guessed that she'd died so horribly.

Mia stood near the head of the coffin. If she reached out, she could touch Alicia's blond hair.

Yellow roses lay all around her inside the coffin and sat in vases at the head and foot of it.

"I'm sorry," Mia whispered. "I wish I could change things. If I could, I'd go back to last night and do everything differently so that you wouldn't be dead anymore."

Mia leaned closer. She placed her hand on the edge of the coffin.

Pain shot through her palm.

I jabbed myself with one of the yellow roses, Mia realized. She gently tried to pull the thorns out of her skin.

The stem tightened around her hand. The thorns sank deeper into her flesh.

Something red pulsed through the delicate veins of the flower. It spread quickly, staining the petals. Soon the whole flower had turned the color of blood.

Mia's blood.

"No," she whispered. "What are you?"

She stepped away from the coffin. She grabbed the blossom and yanked as hard as she could. She hurled the rose onto the carpet.

The rose lifted its blossom head, shaking it to and fro. Mia backed away from it and bumped into the coffin.

She felt thorns jab into her back. Digging through her dress.

"Get off me!" she cried.

She swung her arm wildly. She reached behind her, trying to pull the roses off her back.

Crash!

She knocked a vase of the yellow roses onto the carpet. Water and roses spilled across the floor.

Mia felt a tug on her skirt. The roses were crawling up her body.

This can't be real! she thought. It can't be happening!

Mia dashed toward the door. She tripped over a footstool and went sprawling onto the floor.

A rose wrapped around her ankle. She could feel its thorns pushing deep into her flesh.

In an instant, the rose turned from yellow to red. Mia's blood pulsed through the flower.

"Get away from me!" she cried.

The roses swarmed over her. Changing from yellow to red as they drank her blood.

Mia felt suddenly sleepy. So sleepy.

The room began to tilt around her. The scent of the roses filled the room. So strong, so sweet. She heard a rushing sound in her ears.

It's the sound of my blood rushing through my veins, she realized. Rushing into the roses.

Her vision began to grow dim. Soon, there would be only blackness.

Chapter Eighteen

Mia's eyelids grew heavy, and heavier still.

The sweet smell of the roses filled her with every breath.

I can't fall asleep, she thought. If I do, they will drink all my blood.

But she felt so tired. Her eyelids drifted closed.

I'll die, Mia thought.

Pain exploded through her. One of the roses had pierced the tender skin of her throat.

129

The white-hot agony forced her awake.

Mia yanked the rose off her throat. She crushed it between her hands. Blood-red petals fluttered to the floor.

Mia struggled to her feet. She ripped a rose off her shoulder and threw it to the ground.

She smashed the rose under her foot, and blood spattered across the floor.

My blood, Mia thought. Her stomach turned over.

Mia pulled another rose off herself, and smashed it. Then another, and another.

She had to get out of there! She knew she wouldn't get another chance.

She staggered toward the door. A few more steps, and she'd be out.

But the roses smelled so sweet. And she was so tired.

Couldn't she rest for just a moment?

No! Mia thought. They'll kill you. Keep moving.

Mia took another step. Then another.

Her hand closed on the cool metal of the door latch. There! She made it!

She stumbled out into the hall, then slammed the door behind her.

Her knees buckled. She leaned against

the wall and slid down until she was sitting on the floor.

She gulped huge breaths of fresh air. The drowsy, sleepy feeling was fading. She could think again.

Joanna did this, she realized. Joanna and the others. Her *friends*. They had found a way to use the power without her.

"I've been so stupid," Mia whispered. "They were never my friends. They never really liked me. They only wanted me to help them work spells."

Now that she wouldn't help them anymore, they wanted revenge.

What will they do next? she thought. It could be anything, anything at all.

She had to find out. She had to be prepared. She had to find a way to defend herself against them.

"Mia?"

She looked up to see Clara standing at the end of the hallway. "Mia, are you all right?" she asked.

"I . . . think so," she replied.

Clara hurried down the hall. Her dark eyes were full of concern as she bent over Mia. "Then why are you sitting on the floor?" she demanded.

"I . . . well . . ." Mia began.

What could she say? How could she describe what had happened to her in that room?

"I went in the parlor," she continued at last. "Alicia's coffin is in there. And I got upset."

"Upset?" Clara echoed. "Mia, you're bleeding!"

Mia looked down. Blood streaked her hands. Deep puncture wounds marked her skin.

She thrust her hands into her pockets. "They put some roses in her coffin and in vases around it," Mia told Clara. "I . . . knocked them over by accident. When I tried to catch them, I stuck myself with the thorns."

"Well, why didn't you say so in the first place, you ninny?" Clara demanded. "We'd better clean up in there before Miss Pemberthy finds out."

She started toward the door. Mia grabbed her by the arm and held her back. "No!" she cried. "Don't go in there!"

Clara stared at her. "Why not?"

"It's not safe," Mia blurted out. She shook her head. "I mean, there's a coffin in there!"

"Don't worry, Mia," Clara assured her. "I'm not afraid."

"But—"

Clara pulled free of Mia's grasp and opened the door. Mia ran after her, ready to pull her away again.

But the roses lay unmoving on the carpet.

And they'd turned yellow again!

"What a mess!" Clara exclaimed. "It looks like a battle was fought in here."

Mia gave a shaky laugh. Clara was more right than she could ever have imagined.

It's a good thing you didn't tell the truth about it, she thought. Clara would think you had completely lost your mind.

"Come on, Mia," Clara called.

Mia took a deep breath and followed Clara into the room. "I'll straighten the coffin and sweep, while you pick up the roses," Mia said.

"Are you sure?" Clara asked, frowning. "I thought you were afraid of the coffin."

Mia swallowed hard. "I . . . ah, don't like the smell of roses."

Mia studied the checkerboard. Clara was ahead. Mia needed to find a good move to beat her.

Someone knocked on the door. "It's nine o'clock, girls," Miss Connors called. "Time to turn off the lamp and get to bed."

"Yes, Miss Connors," Clara replied.

The teacher's footsteps went off down the hall. Mia blew out the lamp.

"Why don't we sneak Goliath in tonight?" Clara suggested. "I haven't seen him since the snowstorm."

"That's a good idea," Mia answered.

It had been her fault that they hadn't seen Goliath lately. She'd been so set on keeping Joanna's and the others' friendship that she'd neglected both the cat and Clara.

Well, that wasn't going to happen anymore, she thought. She knew who her true friend was now.

The moment they thought everyone had gone to sleep, Mia and Clara sneaked downstairs. When Mia opened the back door, she found Goliath waiting for them.

Clara scooped him up, and they tiptoed back upstairs. "I wish I had a cat of my own," she said. She set Goliath on the floor between their beds.

Mia dragged a strip of cloth across the

floor for Goliath to chase. He pounced on it with a growl.

Clara giggled. "He's such a ninny!" she said.

"Girls, quiet, please," Miss Connors called from down the hall.

"I thought she'd gone to her room. We're lucky we didn't get caught sneaking Goliath in," Mia whispered.

Clara climbed into bed and pulled Goliath up next to her. "Let's let him stay with us until morning," she said. "We can let him out before breakfast."

"All right," Mia said. She climbed into bed. "Good night, you two."

Mia closed her eyes. She felt exhausted. But she couldn't get comfortable.

She tried lying on her back, then her side, then her stomach. But she couldn't fall asleep.

A board creaked in the hallway. Mia sat bolt upright, her heart pounding.

She heard soft footsteps creeping toward the staircase. And she knew who it was.

The roses hadn't been enough for Joanna and the others. Now, they were going to try again.

"You're evil," she muttered under her

breath. "The power has made you evil!"

Mia wanted to hide under her covers and pretend none of this had happened. But it had.

She wouldn't be safe under the covers. She wouldn't be safe anywhere.

Unless she found a way to stop them.

She had to go. She had to follow them.

Mia covered her face with her hands. "I don't want to do this!" she whispered.

But she had to.

With a sigh, she lowered her hands, glancing over her shoulder at Clara. She and Goliath were sound alseep.

Mia grabbed her cloak and slipped downstairs. She waited in the kitchen a few moments to give the girls time to go inside the barn, then she slipped outside.

She shivered as she hurried over to the barn. Clouds scuttled across the face of the moon. Matching shadows crawled eerily over the ground.

Mia's heart pounded against her ribs as she sneaked to the tack-room window. She was afraid. Afraid to be out here. But more afraid not to know what Joanna and the other girls had planned for her.

Light flickered in the window. They'd lit the candles already.

Mia eased closer. They began to chant. Her throat tightened with fear. What spell were they casting now? What would it do?

What would it bring?

Holding her breath, she peeped through the window. She could see them. They sat in a circle, the book on the floor in the center.

And there were five of them!

That's how they made the roses come to life without her. They had already found another girl to complete the circle. The new girl had her back to the window, so Mia couldn't see her face.

Mia leaned forward, trying to catch the words of the spell. This was a new one. A complicated one. And it felt dark. Dangerous.

They are calling up something evil, Mia thought. And they are going to send it after me.

The rhythm of the chant quickened. She had to stop them! She had to stop them now.

If she could distract them somehow, keep them from finishing that spell . . .

Too late.

The girls uttered the last word of the chant.

Mia's breath caught in her chest.

Something was out there. With her.

Chapter Nineteen

Mia pressed her back against the barn.

What had they called?

She remembered that horrible, misshapen thing that had formed out of the shadows. And the deep claw marks it had left on the tree.

Mia pressed harder against the rough boards behind her. She couldn't tear her gaze away from the woods.

Were the shadows under the trees darker than before?

What had they called?

Mia peered into the darkness. Was something moving out there? Was something watching her?

Mia heard a soft scraping sound on the barn roof. Something was up there!

She spun around, and saw two yellow eyes glowing down at her.

Meowrrr.

Goliath! The cat must have followed her outside.

Mia took a deep breath, then another. She felt her heart begin to slow down.

Had she imagined the danger after all?

No, she decided. The feeling of wrongness was still here.

Goliath jumped lightly down beside her.

Mia picked him up, and he gave a loud meow.

"Shhh," she whispered. "Quiet. Please, be quiet."

He just blinked at her. Cradling him against her shoulder, she slipped into the shadows behind a stack of firewood.

Somewhere out there in the darkness, something waited. Something bad.

Mia didn't know how she knew, but she did. She felt certain the girls' spell had summoned something.

A fine mist of snow whipped along the ground. Above Mia's head, the tree branches creaked and groaned.

Her gaze skipped from shadow to shadow. Watching. Waiting.

She wanted to run back to the house, and safety. But she didn't have the courage to leave her hiding place.

No. She couldn't bear the thought of crossing the open space between the barn and the school, in plain view of . . . whatever was out there.

Mia glanced at the barn window. It was dark. They blew out the candles, she thought. They should be heading back to the school any moment.

Mia set Goliath on top of the woodpile. He rubbed his big head roughly against her arm and meowed.

"Shhh," she whispered. "Do you want to give me away?"

She heard a faint squeak as the barn door opened. She slid along the building and peered around the corner. The girls filed out.

Emily Lloyd. That's who replaced me in the circle, Mia thought.

Emily was the kind of girl who would do

anything she was told. And that's exactly why Joanna picked her, Mia decided.

Mia swallowed hard as she watched them walk toward the schoolhouse with their long cloaks billowing around them. She could hear their shoes crunching in the snow.

Goliath growled low in his throat.

"I don't like them either," Mia whispered.

Goliath growled again. Mia glanced down at him.

He was staring into the woods. Every hair on his body stood on end. His tail was puffed up to twice its normal size. His ears lay flat against his head.

He's afraid, she thought.

"What is it?" Mia whispered. "What do you see?"

Goliath sprang away from her. He raced around the corner of the barn and disappeared.

Mia shivered. I can't stay out here all night, she thought. It's not so far from the barn to the school. I'll just run as fast as I can.

She took a final glance into the woods. "You will be fine," she whispered to herself. "Just go."

Mia raced toward the school. The thick snow dragged at her feet, slowing her down.

"Mia!"

She stopped. Turned. Who was calling her?

"Mia!"

The call was louder now. Frightened. And it had come from the woods.

"Mi-i-i-a-a-a!"

"Clara," Mia whispered. "Oh, no!"

"Help me!" Clara cried. "Someone help me-e-e-e-e!"

Mia raced into the woods. Branches clawed at her cloak and hair as she ran. "Clara, where are you?" she shouted.

"Here. I'm over here," Clara yelled. Her voice sounded high and shrill.

Mia spotted Clara struggling to free herself from a thorny bush.

"Mia, help!" she called.

"I'm coming." Mia panted as she fought her way over to Clara. She reached out to grasp the other girl's hand.

Her fingers passed right through Clara.

Mia stumbled and nearly fell.

Mia tried to catch hold of her friend's cloak. But her hand passed straight through. As if . . . as if Clara had been made of mist.

"Clara?" Mia stammered. "Clara!"

Clara wavered, shimmering like heat off a metal roof.

Then she disappeared.

Clara had been an illusion! Mia realized.

Mia's throat went dry.

This was a trap, she thought. A lure. Created to draw her here, leaving her alone with . . . what?

"Oh, no," she gasped. "Oh, no!"

The snow around her stirred. Puffs of fine powder rose into the air.

But there was no wind tonight.

The snow began to swirl around her. It rose higher and higher.

Mia felt the cold soak into her skin as the snow pressed against her legs.

Run! she ordered herself.

But she couldn't move her legs. The snow formed a wall around them.

Mia tugged at her legs, trying desperately to pull them from the snow.

It was impossible.

She was trapped.

"Help!" she screamed. "Someone! Help me!"

Mia heard a low rumble. She felt the ground tremble under her feet.

She turned her head—and saw an enormous wave of snow rushing toward her.

Chapter Twenty

The snow rose over Mia like a great ocean wave. Then it crashed down on top of her.

She raised her arms to shield herself as the snow poured over her, trapping her in a waist-high frozen blanket.

Mia twisted and jerked, trying to break free. But the snow was too heavy, too tightly packed around her legs.

"Let . . . me . . . get . . . out," she gasped.

The rumbling sound began again. And

another snow wave rose up and swept over Mia.

Now the snow reached her chest. Cold seeped into her flesh.

Another wave of snow slammed down on her. The snow climbed to her chin.

"Help me!" she screamed. "Somebody help me!"

Snow flowed into her mouth. She gasped and coughed.

She tilted her head back, trying to keep her nose clear, but the snow kept pouring down on her.

Until it covered her completely.

Mia clawed frantically at the snow. Her fingers turned numb. But she didn't stop. She couldn't. If she stopped, this mound of snow would be her grave. She kept digging.

Tears ran from her eyes and froze on her cheeks. Her chest burned as she struggled to draw breath. The air was almost gone.

Mia kept clawing through the snow, digging a narrow tunnel above her. Faster, she ordered herself.

She felt a tiny hole open up at the top of the tunnel. Cold air trickled down to her. And she could see a single star up in the night sky.

Mia locked her eyes on the star and kept digging. Dig until you reach the star, she thought.

Mia worked on the hole until it looked big enough for her to fit through. She fought her way up the tunnel, inch by inch.

I'm almost there, she thought. I'm almost out. I'm almost to my star.

The tunnel grew narrower and narrower. Mia dug out more chunks of snow.

But the tunnel didn't feel any wider. It felt smaller.

The snow is moving, she realized. The walls are closing in.

The hole at the top of the tunnel filled with snow—and Mia's star disappeared.

The walls pushed closer. Pressing, squeezing. The snow was so cold, so terribly heavy.

She gasped. The snow shoved against her ribs. It filled her nose and mouth.

I can't breathe, Mia thought. Red patches swam in front of her eyes.

She heard a faint sound through the blanketing snow. What was that?

She strained to hear more. It sounded like a human voice!

Hope burned through her. Had someone

heard her cry for help? Had they come to save her?

The voice came closer. Mia struggled feebly against the walls of snow all around her. If she could only get some room, some breath, she could call out!

Mia burrowed through the thick snow, forcing her cold hands to work faster and faster. I have to make them realize I'm down here, she thought.

Then she heard a high trill of laughter. A girl's laughter.

Mia knew who it was. Joanna. She and the others thought they'd beaten Mia. They thought she would die.

And they were gloating.

Anger pumped heat through her veins. She wasn't about to give up! She struggled upward furiously, kicking and clawing at the snow.

And then her head broke through into the crisp night air!

Mia hauled herself out of the tunnel. She rolled down the side of the snowy mound.

She could feel the snow moving beneath her. She knew it would bury her again if she didn't keep moving.

Mia shoved herself up and staggered forward. She couldn't feel her feet. They were completely numb.

Mia heard a low rumbling sound. It's coming, she thought. The snow is coming.

She stumbled on, shoving her way through the trees. The rumbling grew louder.

She burst out of the woods. Snow came pouring out after her, striking the back of her legs. Mia kept running.

She risked a glance over her shoulder. The snow was retreating, flowing back into the woods.

She made it! She was going to live!

Her teeth chattered as she rushed to the back door of the school. Her hands wouldn't stop trembling as she turned the doorknob.

Mia lurched inside, and shut the door behind her. The big iron stove still radiated heat into the room.

Mia rushed to it and held her numb hands out to its warmth. Slowly, the chill was driven from her body.

I must find a way to stop Joanna and the others, Mia thought. They will never leave me alone.

She was too tired to think. Tomorrow. She'd deal with them tomorrow.

She eased the kitchen door open and listened. The house was quiet. She slipped out into the hallway and scurried toward the staircase.

I'm glad Clara is upstairs, Mia thought. It didn't matter that she was asleep. Mia just didn't want to be alone right now.

She started up the stairs. Her wet petticoat clung uncomfortably to her ankles, and she bent to pull it free.

When she straightened up, she saw three dark figures standing at the top of the stairs.

They stepped forward, into the faint moonlight slanting through the far window.

Joanna. Irene. Phoebe.

They stared at Mia with cold, hate-filled eyes. Joanna held the spell book cradled in her arms. Even from here, Mia could feel its power.

Its evil power. It had turned *them* evil somehow, Mia knew. Even Irene, who had been so timid and gentle.

"Hello, Mia," Joanna said. "We've been waiting for you."

Chapter Twenty-one

What were they going to do to her? Mia whirled and ran down the stairs.

Anabel and Emily, the new member of the circle, stepped into the hall. They blocked the bottom of the staircase.

Mia didn't slow her pace. She flew down the stairs and pushed past Anabel and Emily.

She dashed into the kitchen and over to the back door. She jerked on the handle, but the door stuck.

Panting, Mia pulled with all her strength. She forced the door open an inch, and then another inch. Then the door slammed shut again.

She heard soft footsteps in the hall outside.

The kitchen door creaked slowly open.

Joanna and the others stood in the doorway, staring at her.

Mia's heart pounded. How could she have been so stupid? How could she have ever thought these girls were her friends?

"You were spying on us tonight," Joanna accused.

"I wasn't going to tell anyone anything," Mia protested. "I only wanted to know what you had planned."

"It isn't any of your business," Joanna told her. "Remember, *you* were the one who didn't want to be part of our group anymore."

Mia turned to Emily. "You're in danger, Emily," she said. "The spells are evil. One girl has already died because of them."

"That was an accident, and you know it!" Joanna snapped.

Mia shook her head. "Tell her about Alicia, Joanna. Tell her about the spiders."

Anabel pushed to the front of the group. Her face twisted with anger as she glared at Mia. "You're just mean and selfish." She spat out the words. "You tried to spoil things for the rest of us, and now you're mad that it didn't work."

"It isn't like that at all!" Mia protested.

"Oh, why are we talking to you at all?" Joanna cried. "You *did* try to spoil it. But we found somebody new, and now we're going to deal with you! Form the circle!"

The girls linked hands.

Mia knew she had very little time left.

"I'll scream," she warned them. "Miss Pemberthy will come."

"Let her come." Joanna sneered. "We control the power of the spell book. If she tries to interfere, we'll deal with *her*, too. Let them all come. They'll be sorry if they do."

"Are you all so willing to kill and kill and kill?" Mia cried. "Are you, Irene? Are you, Emily?"

They ignored her. The girls began to chant.

One against five. Mia, just Mia, against the evil power of the spell book. How could she possibly fight that?

The girls' chant grew louder.

Dishes rattled on their shelves. Pots and pans clattered against each other. Utensils banged inside the drawers.

A saucer came whizzing toward Mia's head. She dodged it. It slammed into the door behind her and shattered.

Then the whole wall of cabinets seemed to explode. The doors flew open with a crash. Dishes, cups, gravy boats, forks, spoons, and knives all flew at Mia.

Mia flung up her arms to protect her face. A cup bounced off her hip. A plate slammed into her forearm. A knife glanced off her shoulder, and Mia felt a hot spurt of blood.

A platter banged into her shin, and she skidded down on one knee.

"Make it stop!" she shrieked.

Then she saw the cleaver.

Light glittered off its deadly metal blade as it whirled and spun. . . .

Straight toward her.

Chapter Twenty-two

Mia threw herself to the floor. The cleaver whirled toward her.

And missed. But it was close, so close! She felt the breeze it made as it went by.

Mia crawled toward the kitchen table. Maybe it would offer her some protection.

The cleaver spun around in a tight circle. Then it slashed down again.

Mia rolled to the side. The blade nicked her shoulder.

The cleaver whistled through the air.

Mia tried to roll again—and slammed into the wall.

She stared up at the cleaver. It was coming back again. Right toward her face.

"No!" Mia cried, flinging her hand up.

The cleaver flew away from her, as if she'd caught the handle and thrown it.

Thunk!

The blade sunk deep into the far wall.

The girls stopped chanting in mid-word.

They stood staring at the cleaver, their eyes wide with shock. Then they turned to look at Mia.

"How did you do that?" Anabel demanded shrilly.

Mia shook her head helplessly. She hadn't done anything to the cleaver. She hadn't even *tried* to do anything. She'd only wanted to live.

"It doesn't matter," Joanna interrupted sharply. She held the book up in front of her. "Finish the spell!"

"Are you willing to kill again, Irene?" Mia cried. "Are you, Emily? Think about what you are doing."

The two glanced at each other. Mia knew they were uncertain. Even Phoebe and Anabel hesitated.

"She is dangerous to us," Joanna said. "She knows our secrets, and we can't trust her anymore."

"But I won't tell, I promise," Mia begged.

They ignored her. They began to chant again.

A heavy iron skillet rose off the stove. Knives and forks flew out of the sink, dripping sudsy water. The teapot and two teacups swooped off the kitchen table.

And then they hurled themselves at Mia.

A teacup hit her in the temple, staggering her. Then a fork stabbed into her wrist. She screamed in pain and terror.

"Noooo!" she shrieked. She raised her arms to shield herself—and blue-white fire exploded from her hands.

The teapot shattered in mid-air.

The skillet thumped down onto the floor. The utensils dropped with a clatter.

Mia stood frozen in shock. The flames swept back into her hands and disappeared.

The room was completely silent. Mia could almost hear her own heart beating. The girls just stood and stared at her.

Then Emily wrenched away from the circle and ran. Mia pointed at her. The kitchen rug jerked out from under the girl's feet. She gave a high squeal as she fell. The rug wrapped itself around her.

Only her feet could be seen. They kicked frantically, while her muffled screams went on and on.

Anabel and Irene slowly backed away.

"No," Mia said softly.

Two of the wooden kitchen chairs rose into the air.

One chair flew at Anabel. The other at Irene. The chairs shoved the girls against the wall.

Then the chairs stabbed their legs into the walls, trapping the girls beneath them.

"No, no, no, no," Anabel moaned.

Irene squeezed her eyes shut. "This isn't happening," she whispered to herself.

I'm doing this! Mia realized. I'm making these things happen!

And she was doing it alone. She could feel the power racing through her. Her whole body tingled with it.

Ready to be used.

Slowly, she turned to look at Phoebe and Joanna. They knew. Maybe they could see the power in her, or feel it.

Phoebe opened her mouth, then shut it.

Her knees buckled. And she slumped to the floor.

She fainted, Mia realized.

That only left Joanna. Her enemy. This was all Joanna's fault. None of the others would have turned on her if Joanna hadn't told them to.

"I never liked you," Joanna said defiantly. "If we hadn't needed five girls to make the circle, I wouldn't even have talked to you!"

"You are evil," Mia said. "It's your fault that Alicia's dead. The rest of us disliked her because she was so rude to us all the time. But you hated her. You hated her because she was more popular than you. Even with the teachers."

"That's not true!" Joanna cried. "The teachers only liked her because her father gave money to the school. There isn't anyone in this school who's sorry she's dead!"

Mia shook her head. Even Clara had felt sorry for Alicia, and Alicia had been nastier to her than anyone else. But there wasn't any point in telling Joanna that.

"Give me the book, Joanna," she said.

Joanna clutched the book tightly against her.

"You can't have the power anymore,

Joanna," Mia told her. "It's too dangerous. The book needs to be destroyed."

Joanna's eyes narrowed. "Oh, is that so? And who is going to dare take it from me?"

"I am." Mia held out her hand. "I don't want to hurt you, Joanna. Just give me the book."

"No!" Tears ran down Joanna's face. "I can't give up the power. Besides, if you destroy the book, you'll lose *your* power, too!"

"I don't care," Mia told her. "I wish I'd never seen that horrible thing."

She moved toward Joanna. The other girl's eyes went wide with fear and rage. She held the book so tightly that her knuckles turned white.

"Stay away from me," she cried. "I'm warning you!"

Mia pointed at Joanna. "Give me the book!"

Joanna hurled the book at Mia.

Blue-white fire shot from Mia's hands.

The book exploded into flame.

Mia flew backward. She struck her head on the kitchen table.

And the world went black.

Chapter Twenty-three

Mia opened her eyes. The kitchen ceiling seemed to be spinning.

Then she blinked, and the spinning stopped.

Every muscle in her body hurt. "Ohhhhh," she groaned, forcing herself to sit up.

The spell book lay in shreds on the floor. Wisps of smoke rose from it.

I must have blacked out for a moment, Mia realized. She pushed herself to her feet and stared around the room.

The other girls were all unconscious. But to her relief, they didn't seem to be hurt.

Mia unrolled the carpet from around Emily. She pulled the chairs away from Anabel and Irene, and the girls slumped to the floor.

Then she went to Joanna. Joanna lay facedown. She moaned softly when Mia knelt beside her.

"Are you all right?" Mia whispered. She rolled Joanna onto her back.

Joanna's eyes flew open. She sat bolt upright.

Mia flinched back in surprise.

Joanna stared straight out, her face expressionless.

Mia took her by the shoulders and shook her gently. "Joanna? Can you talk to me? Are you feeling well?"

A low chuckle erupted from deep in Joanna's throat.

Mia slid away from her.

Joanna's chuckles grew louder and wilder until she was shrieking with laughter. Her face remained without expression. Her green eyes—usually so alert—stared blankly.

"Stop it," Mia pleaded. "Stop!"

The kitchen door banged open and Miss Pemberthy raced into the room. "What on earth is going on in h—" She broke off, her mouth falling open as she saw the wreckage.

"Joanna! Joanna Kershaw!" she ordered. "Stop laughing, young lady. Immediately!"

But Joanna didn't stop.

Mia didn't think she *could* stop.

The headmistress went to her and grabbed her by the shoulders. "Joanna!" she cried, shaking her. "What is the matter with you?"

Joanna just kept laughing. She threw back her head, tossing her red curls in Miss Pemberthy's shocked face, and shrieked with laughter. Her whole body shook as she laughed and laughed.

Miss Pemberthy looked at Mia. "You'd better tell me exactly what happened here," she ordered.

"Ah . . . I don't know. She seems to have . . . gone mad," Mia told the headmistress. "She started screaming and smashing everything. And then she knocked the other girls unconscious."

It was a ridiculous story. But it would be

easier for Miss Pemberthy to believe than the truth, Mia decided.

"This is terrible," Miss Pemberthy wailed, letting go of her hold on Joanna. Joanna tumbled to the floor. Her shrieks of laughter dissolved into hysterical giggles.

"Oh, the poor thing! Mia, go upstairs and fetch the other teachers. I'm going to need help here."

Mia raced up the stairs. Now that everything was over, Mia started to shake. It had been so awful! Alicia was dead, and now Joanna had gone insane.

And all because of the power.

The power. It hadn't gone away when the book was destroyed.

Mia could feel it still inside her. She could use it if she wanted to. But she didn't want it.

"I'm never going to use it again," she vowed. "Never, never, never!"

Mia and Clara stood at their window and watched as the five carriages drove off, taking Joanna, Irene, Phoebe, Anabel, and Emily away. Their parents had come to take them home.

"Poor Joanna," Mia murmured. "Poor

Mrs. Kershaw. She cried from the moment she got here and was still sobbing as she climbed back into her carriage."

"Can you blame her?" Clara asked.

Mia shook her head. She felt tears sting her eyes. She never wanted to hurt Joanna. She never wanted to hurt anyone. She just wanted them to leave her alone.

She sighed, thinking of Joanna's pale, blank face. Once Joanna had finally stopped laughing, she drifted into some silent world all her own.

"It's been a week, and Joanna still never said a word," Mia murmured. "She hasn't even recognized anybody."

"I heard Miss Pemberthy tell one of the teachers that all those girls are a little, well, strange," Clara told her. "They told the most incredible stories about what happened. That's why she's sending them home, too."

"What kind of stories?" Mia asked, trying her best to hide her sudden alarm.

"Oh, insane things," Clara replied. "Flying chairs, and rugs that swallowed people up—"

"That *is* madness," Mia agreed. "But now everything is back to normal."

"Thank goodness," Clara said. "I'd hate to go down to the kitchen for a drink of water some night and get attacked by a vicious throw rug."

They both laughed. For the first time since Mia had felt the power, she wasn't afraid.

It was over. Everything was going to be all right now.

That night, Mia began to drift off to sleep the moment she crawled into bed. It felt so good under the blankets—warm and safe.

Then she heard a sound that made her skin prickle.

Chanting.

Someone was chanting somewhere in the house.

But it's over! Mia thought. No one else knew about the spell book, or chanting spells!

Mia squeezed her eyes shut and pulled her pillow over her head. She didn't want to be afraid again.

But she couldn't pretend she didn't hear.

She had to go look.

Mia climbed out of bed and threw her dressing gown around her shoulders. I have to make sure nothing bad happens, she thought. I have to make sure no one else gets hurt. She let herself out into the hall.

Where was the chanting coming from? She stopped to listen.

The attic, she thought. Someone is chanting in the attic.

Mia took a deep breath and hurried down the hall to the attic staircase. She opened the door and tiptoed up the narrow stairs. The wooden steps felt cold against her bare feet.

Mia hesitated outside the attic door. Then she eased it open.

The moment she did, the chanting ended. Mia glanced around the long, low room.

"Who's there?" she whispered into the shadows.

Silence.

She started to turn away. Maybe I dreamed it, Mia thought. I was in bed when I heard the chanting. Maybe I was still half asleep when I came up here. Maybe . . .

A cold wash of air poured over her. And a sudden, strong feeling of dread filled her.

There was power here.

But Joanna and the others are gone! she told herself. The book is destroyed!

"Mia."

The voice was soft and warm. And somehow . . . inhuman.

It was evil.

Mia's legs felt weak and rubbery.

It's the voice I heard chanting, she thought. The voice that lured me into the attic.

"Mia."

Mia peered into the room. Moonlight shone faintly over the far wall.

She gasped. Her breath felt as though it had turned to ice in her chest.

The wood, she thought. It's *moving*.

Mia heard a creaking, groaning sound, and the wall began to stretch and bulge. Bumps and hollows appeared in the wood.

It . . . it's forming a face, Mia realized. An enormous face.

The eyes opened.

Chapter Twenty-four

It sees me, Mia thought. She slowly backed away.

"Mia."

It called her by name. It knew her.

"Mia," the voice called. "Miaaaa!"

The face stretched toward her.

The attic filled with an awful stench. A smell of death and decay. The smell of decomposing bodies.

Mia felt her stomach cramp. She swallowed hard.

She whirled and ran for the stairs.

The graveyard stench grew stronger. The smell of rotting flesh filled her mouth, her nose, her lungs.

Mia scrambled down the stairs. She dashed through the door and into the hallway. She slammed the door shut behind her.

She stepped into the hallway. Her foot sunk into the floor.

The solid oak planks were turning to liquid beneath her.

Mia slipped deeper into the floor. It felt like thick mud around her legs.

She fought her way forward.

Then the floor began to harden again.

She couldn't move. She couldn't take another step.

She was trapped. Helpless.

Who could be doing this? she thought frantically. The others were all gone. The spell book was gone!

Then she heard footsteps. Her breath came in sharp, frightened rasps as the footsteps moved closer and closer.

Who was it? *What* was it?

Mia twisted from side to side, trying to pry herself loose. She clawed at the wood with her fingers. Pain shot up her arm as one of her fingernails ripped away.

There was no way out

A shadow moved on the wall at the far end of the hallway. It rippled over every bump and board. Mia whimpered.

Then someone stepped into sight. Mia's breath went out in a sigh that left her limp.

Clara.

"Thank goodness!" Mia cried. "I'm so glad to see you, Clara! Come help me out of here!"

Clara shook her head. "I thought you were my friend," she said.

"I am!" Mia cried.

"You lied to me. And now you're going to pay."

Chapter Twenty-five

"I don't understand," Mia whispered.

"I have the power," Clara said. "I've had it all along. Just like you."

"What?" Mia exclaimed. "Why didn't you tell me?"

"You kept secrets from me, so I kept secrets from you," Clara answered.

I have to get away from her, Mia thought. She jerked back and forth, trying to pull her legs free.

"You and I were the special ones," Clara

said. "The spell book released the power inside us. The others were so stupid! They didn't realize they had no power of their own!"

"But they trapped me in a wall of snow out in the woods," Mia protested. "They made the roses on Alicia's coffin attack me!"

"No," Clara said softly. "I did. Just as I made the kitchen knives and forks attack you."

"You!"

"Yes, Mia," Clara replied. "Me. Clumsy old Clara. I found the book one day in Joanna's room. The power came to me the moment I laid my hands on it. And that's how it happened to you, too. Who knows why we were chosen?"

"How could you do those terrible things to me?" Mia cried. "I thought you were my friend!"

Clara's face looked pale and pinched in the dimness. "We were the ones with the gift," she answered. "We were meant to be friends. But you ruined it."

"How can you say that?" Mia protested. "I always defended you when Alicia said unkind things to you."

"You said you were my friend," Clara told her. "But you never confided in me. And you never once thought to include me in your little group."

I must keep her talking until I can find a way to escape, Mia thought.

"I asked them to let you join us," Mia protested. "It wasn't my fault that the others wouldn't allow it. And I couldn't tell you what we were doing. I swore on the power of the spell book that I wouldn't."

"So you made your choice," Clara sneered. "And you chose them. I was only good enough to be your friend when there was no one better around."

"That's not true," Mia cried. "Think of all the fun we've had. Remember the nights we snuck Goliath up to our room."

"You chose Joanna and those other ninnies over me," Clara retorted. "But your precious friends are gone now, aren't they?"

Her eyes glittered with hate as she glared at Mia. "Now it is your turn to die."

"No!" Mia screamed.

Clara's power burst free. Splinters of wood sprayed everywhere in a flash of blue-white light.

Clara's mouth twisted into a snarl. Mia could feel the power radiating from her roommate. Cold. Evil.

Clara spread her arms wide. Shadows gathered around her. They seethed and coiled, growing thicker with every moment.

And then she pointed at Mia.

The inky shadows slithered across the floor toward her. Fast, so terribly fast!

Mia screamed as they poured over her. She could feel them sucking the strength out of her. Draining her energy. Feeding on her.

"Kill her!" Clara shrieked. "Kill her!"

Mia had to do something. She could feel the power inside her, waiting. This time, she wasn't afraid to use it.

Help me! she screamed in her mind. Save me!

She felt a tingling sensation in her forehead. A rushing sound filled her ears.

Then the power surged through her in a great fountain. It burned through her veins.

Blue-white bolts of lightning shot out of Mia's body. They slashed through the shadows that covered her.

A hot smell of burning flesh stung her nose.

The shadows twitched and jerked, and a thin, inhuman shriek echoed through the hall.

The shadows recoiled. They flowed back to Clara and swirled around her feet.

They moved up Clara's body. Wrapping themselves around her. Covering her face.

The shadows drew her into the air. They tightened around Clara. Squeezing her.

Clara uttered a strangled scream.

Mia covered her mouth with her hands to keep from screaming herself.

Tiny red droplets began to patter down on the wooden floor.

Clara's blood.

Mia shuddered. She watched the red droplets splash onto the floor.

Drip. Drip. Drip.

"Enough," Mia whispered. She raised her hand and pointed at the shadows. A single blue-white flame flickered to life on her fingertip.

"Go," she said. "Go back to where you came from."

The shadows disappeared instantly.

"And don't ever come back," she added.

Was it over? Mia felt a sob of relief escape her throat. Was it truly over?

Chapter Twenty-six

The carriage rolled to a stop in front of the schoolhouse steps. Mia handed her case to the driver, then turned to face Miss Pemberthy.

"Are you sure you won't change your mind about leaving, Mia?" the headmistress asked.

"I'm sure," Mia replied.

"I know you are distraught over Clara's disappearance. But you might regret your decision later," Miss Pemberthy said. "Take more time to think it over."

"I don't need any more time," Mia told her. "I want to go home."

The headmistress sighed. "Very well, dear. Good-bye, and have a safe journey."

Mia turned toward the carriage. Then she swung around to look at the headmistress again. "Miss Pemberthy, do you ever wonder if those old stories about Mrs. Reade practicing the dark arts are true? Did she leave any family here? Did they . . . ?"

"No!"

A frightened expression crossed Miss Pemberthy's face. Then she shook her head firmly. "Goodness, Mia! I told you before, the dark arts do not exist. And none of Mrs. Reade's family remained in this town. I wish you would forget all about Emma Reade."

Mia sighed. She couldn't tell the truth about what had happened here. No one would believe it. And perhaps that was for the best.

"Good-bye, Miss Pemberthy," Mia said.

She climbed into the carriage and settled back against the cushions. The driver called to the horses and they started forward.

Mia stared out the window until the

school disappeared from sight.

"Good-bye, Broad River," Mia muttered. "I won't miss you."

Her parents didn't know she was coming home. But she didn't care. Nothing could keep her in this town. Nothing could ever make her come back.

But the power. . . .

Mia shivered.

No matter how far she traveled, the power would always be inside her.

I will never use it, Mia promised herself. Never.

Unless I have no other choice.

The terror never ends.
Turn the page to enter the . . .
CHAMBER OF FEAR

FEAR STREET SAGAS® #12

Coming May 1998

There were so many nights I could not sleep in the orphanage. So many nights when bad dreams woke me.

I would climb out of bed and light the stub of a candle. Then I would open my locket and stare down at the tiny portrait inside.

The woman in the portrait was beautiful. Her shining hair was a rich blond, like mine. Her eyes were the blue of a troubled sea. Her smile was soft, but sad. So incredibly sad.

As though she knew a terrible secret.

I could not remember her, but I knew she was my mother. She died when I was two years old. No one would tell me how.

On those nights, I would study her face in the flickering candlelight.

And wonder about her. And miss her.

Even though I did not remember her.

And I would think about my father. He died before I was born. I did not know what he looked like. No one had painted a portrait of him.

But I knew he had been a carpenter. Someone said he built coffins. The thought always made me shudder.

I would imagine the people who lay in the coffins he built. Dead people. Cold people. I could almost feel their icy fingers running down my spine.

Then I would clutch the locket and fill my mind with my mother's face. Until I felt warm and safe.

Memories of my mother always made me feel safe.

Until I turned sixteen. And I learned the truth about my mother.

I discovered the secret behind her sad smile.

I came to understand that evil lurked within shadows. That magic was not simply an illusion performed on a stage.

And that we must constantly fear what we cannot see.

Enchanted, New York, 1845

"**M**rs. Hadel would like to see you in her office," Miss Jackson told me. "Immediately."

All the girls seated at the long wooden table stared at me. "Carolyn is in trouble," someone whispered.

I rose from the table, leaving my meal unfinished. I hurried from the room. My skirt and petticoats swished along the hard-wood floor.

As I moved down the hallway toward Mrs. Hadel's office, my heart began to pound.

You haven't done anything wrong, I told myself. There is no need to feel so nervous.

But my hand shook as I knocked on the heavy oak door.

"Come in!" Mrs. Hadel called.

I pushed open the door and stepped into Mrs. Hadel's neat office. "You wanted to see me?" I asked.

Mrs. Hadel smiled at me. I forced myself to smile back.

If I had a grandmother, I want her to look like Mrs. Hadel. Her white hair was piled into a soft bun on top of her head. And all the smiles she'd given to frightened orphan girls over the years had carved wrinkles at the corners of eyes.

She motioned me over to her with a slender hand. "Come and sit down, Carolyn. I have wonderful news."

Although she said her news was wonderful, she sounded worried.

I sat in the stiff leather chair in front of her mahogany desk.

Mrs. Hadel picked up her pen, then set it down. She moved her paperweight so it sat precisely in the center of her desk.

She is even more anxious than I am, I realized.

Mrs. Hadel cleared her throat. "How shall

I begin?" she murmured to herself. Then she leaned toward me.

"Carolyn, when your mother died, she was in the employment of a man called Mr. Fier. He has always taken an interest in you. Over the years, he has often stopped by the orphanage to check on your progress and make certain you were well."

"I don't understand. I have never seen him. He has never spoken to me, never . . ." My voice trailed off.

"Perhaps he would have found it too painful," Mrs. Hadel told me. She sighed. "Mr. Fier always blamed himself for your mother's death," she said.

A tiny gasp escaped my throat.

"Her death was an accident, of course," Mrs. Hadel added quickly. "I believe Mr. Fier felt making certain you were well taken care of was something he could do for your mother."

Mrs. Hadel gathered the sheets of paper scattered over her desk. She formed them into a neat pile. "Today, Mr. Fier has made you a most generous offer. He would like you to come and work for him."

My stomach felt as though it had fallen to the floor. "Work for him?" I squeaked.

Mrs. Hadel nodded briskly. "Isn't that wonderful?"

I shook my head. "I don't understand. Why has he come forward now? Why is he willing to take me in now, after all these years?"

"You are sixteen, Carolyn. Too old to stay in the orphanage," Mrs. Hadel explained. "When Mr. Fier learned I was hoping to find a position for you, he offered you a job as a servant in his home."

"What would I do for him?" I asked.

"What all servants do," Mrs. Hadel said. "Dust, sweep, polish." She added more gently, "There are no great secrets to being a house servant. Just remember to do exactly as you're told, and don't ask too many questions."

I tried to imagine my new life, working for Mr. Fier.

"So I would go to his house during the day, then return here every night?" I asked hesitantly.

"Oh, no, no, no," Mrs. Hadel exclaimed, clucking her tongue against her teeth.

She pushed back her chair and stood. She set a scarred brown suitcase on the desk. "Mr. Fier brought this valise over so you could pack your things. You will live and work in his home, Owlhurst."

I pushed myself to my feet. My legs felt as though they could barely hold me upright.

"Mrs. Hadel, I had hoped to stay at the orphanage and teach," I reminded her.

"I know, dear, but we have no positions here. If you cannot accept Mr. Fier's offer, I will have to send you to the textile mill."

The textile mill! I had heard horror tales about the mills. Women and children worked from dawn until dusk, seventy hours a week or more.

Mrs. Hadel patted the suitcase. "Go pack your belongings."

I watched her pull a white lace handkerchief from her pocket. She turned away from me slightly, but I saw her wipe a tear from the corner of her eye.

I realized then that my leaving saddened her. For her sake, I forced myself to smile.

"Thank you, Mrs. Hadel. I'm certain I will be very happy working for Mr. Fier."

She sniffed and wiped her nose with the handkerchief. When she looked at me, new tears brimmed in her eyes. "I'm sure you will be, my dear. Happiness comes to those who look for it." She patted me on the shoulder. "Now hurry along. Mr. Fier is expecting you to be at his home promptly at two o'clock. First impressions are very important."

I wrapped my trembling fingers around the handle of the worn leather suitcase and carried it out of Mrs. Hadel's office.

I leaned against the wall outside her door, and took a deep breath.

I was going to work for a man I did not know, in the house where my mother had died.

A chill slithered along my spine. No one had ever told me how my mother had died. Mrs. Hadel said it was not in the orphanage records. Now, after all these years, I might learn the truth about her death.

But after all these years, did I really want to know?

I slowly made my way down the hall. I trudged up the stairs to the long, narrow room where I slept with nine other girls.

I slung the suitcase onto my bed and opened it.

Liza Johnson rushed into the room. She had always been my dearest friend. "What did Mrs. Hadel want?" she asked.

"She found work for me," I answered. "I am leaving this afternoon."

"Oh, Carolyn. I am going to miss you so much," Liza exclaimed. "Did you get a teaching position? You must tell me everything."

Liza and I often talked about what our futures would hold. She knew I dreamed of being a teacher. And I knew her dream—to marry a wealthy man.

Tears burned behind my eyelids. "No, I am going to be a servant," I told her.

"Maybe you could run away—" Liza began.

"What would I do then?" I interrupted. "Starve? Freeze to death?"

Liza stared at the floor. "I'm sorry," she said. "I didn't think." She folded my second-best dress and handed it to me. "Who will you be working for?" she asked.

"Mr. Fier," I told her.

Liza grabbed my arm. "You can't," she gasped. "You must not go to that house!" She gave a small shudder. "I've heard stories about the Fiers. Horrible stories."

She tightened her grip, her fingers digging into me. "Another girl from the orphanage went to work for Mr. Fier years ago." I could hear her voice shaking. "No one ever saw her again."

Liza held my gaze, her eyes wide. "Mr. Fier murdered her!"

About R.L. Stine

R.L. Stine is the best-selling author in America. He has written more than one hundred scary books for young people, all of them bestsellers.

His series include *Fear Street, Ghosts of Fear Street,* and the *Fear Street Sagas*.

Bob grew up in Columbus, Ohio. Today he lives in New York City with his wife, Jane, his son, Matt, and his dog, Nadine.